Christmas N

Two hospitals, four

Great Southern Hospital in London and
Great Northern Hospital in Edinburgh are very special
places. Their close working relationship allows them
to share their considerable talents and world-class
knowledge, from transplant and reconstructive
surgery to neurosurgery and cutting-edge cancer
research. As the festive season begins, and the
sparkle of fairy lights fills the hospital gardens,
staff will be saving lives—and falling in love!

Immerse yourself in the warmth and romance
of the season with...

Tamsin and Max's story
Festive Fling with the Surgeon by Karin Baine

Lauren and Oliver's story
A Mistletoe Marriage Reunion by Louisa Heaton

Skye and Jay's story
Melting Dr. Grumpy's Frozen Heart by Scarlet Wilson

Poppy and Dylan's story
Neurosurgeon's IVF Mix-Up Miracle by Annie Claydon

All available now!

MELTING
DR. GRUMPY'S
FROZEN HEART

SCARLET WILSON

MEDICAL ROMANCE

Special thanks and acknowledgment are given to Scarlet Wilson for her contribution to the Christmas North and South miniseries.

Harlequin®
MEDICAL
ROMANCE

Recycling programs for this product may not exist in your area.

ISBN-13: 978-1-335-94268-5

Melting Dr. Grumpy's Frozen Heart

Copyright © 2024 by Harlequin Enterprises ULC

Harlequin Enterprises ULC
22 Adelaide St. West, 41st Floor
Toronto, Ontario M5H 4E3, Canada
www.Harlequin.com

Printed in U.S.A.

To my darling sister, Jennifer Mary Dickson.
Thank you for being my biggest writing cheerleader.
Will love you and miss you forever. x

CHAPTER ONE

SKYE CAMPBELL WAS BUZZING—literally. She could feel the hum in the air around her. As she walked along the frosty Edinburgh pavement, she smiled in pleasure at the crunch of her steps. She loved this time of year. And Edinburgh did it so well.

Even though it was mid-November, the large Christmas tree that sat near the Scott Monument was already up and decorated in shades of purple, pink and silver. The Edinburgh Christmas market started this weekend, and her Christmas shopping was part way done. Skye only shopped online for things she couldn't find in the shops. Whilst others hated the busyness of the shops at Christmas, she absolutely loved it. There was nothing nicer than watching people buying gifts for their loved ones, puzzling between colours or styles, sniffing samples of perfume in the department stores, or staring at the dazzling array of trainers in a sports shop. She was here for all that.

The Great Northern Hospital was lit up before her with a warm glow. Seven floors of glass, which had been specially constructed to allow patients to see out, but no one could see in. The effect from outside gave a tinged yellow and orange colour like a warm hug. She loved it. If she could meet the architect, she would shake their hand. She gave a sideways glance to Edinburgh Castle in the distance, proudly sitting on its ancient volcano site. She did this every morning, and today there was a hint of white around it. The temperature had dropped suddenly overnight and it seemed like Scotland had remembered it was the most wonderful time of the year.

As the main doors of the hospital slid open before her, her stomach gave a little flip. The whole main entrance was now decorated for Christmas. She'd been campaigning for it since the first of November, so she was glad they'd finally caved. Truth was, it was likely they'd caved to coincide with the city's decorations outside.

White fairy lights were everywhere. A giant tree was cordoned off and could be seen from the few floors above that overlooked the main reception.

'Morning.' Skye waved to Ellis, who sat behind the reception desk, as she headed over to the lifts. She joined the lift with Max Robertson, the very serious paediatric surgeon. She shot him a smile, which he almost returned.

A few minutes later she was striding down the corridor towards her office. She was a tiny bit nervous this morning. She was continually driven in her job as an oncology doctor and researcher. Losing her father to the disease during her medical training had made her realise which direction she wanted to take.

Her friends joked about her being a double doctor. Being a doctor of medicine as well as a doctor of research had meant hard work. Long days and long nights. But she'd been used to that when she'd helped nurse her father towards the end. Other students had been partying. Enjoying the student and hospital social life. Skye had been exactly where she should have been—with her family. And part of the reason she was so determined to make this new project work was due to the subject matter. Time.

Her new ground-breaking study aimed to predict the growth of cancer. It didn't sound pleasant. But anyone who'd worked as an oncologist knew that the first question a patient asked was how long they had. And it was a question a doctor could rarely answer with any confidence. It was always a best guess.

With a new wave of technology, and several early studies, Skye's premise was that AI—artificial intelligence—could help answer that question. It held promise. The battle against cancer was fought on many levels, and hers—the art of learning about the disease and its progression—was only one.

The only downside was she'd just learned that world-renowned oncologist Jay Bannerman was temporarily transferring up from Great Southern Hospital in London. He was going supervise her research for the next six weeks. She needed someone with his credentials to sign off on the next stage of the project. He had huge credibility, and his patients loved him. He'd led lots of cancer studies in the past. But there was a downside—from reputation alone, and whispers from their sister hospital, he was not-so-secretly known as Dr Grumpy.

Skye was more than a little worried. He didn't really fit with her personality type. She always tried to be positive, and tried to bring out the best in people around her. Her colleagues had nicknamed her Miss Sunshine and she didn't mind it one bit.

But a research supervisor for this project was essential. Her original supervisor had gone into hospital for a knee replacement and was expected to be off for six weeks. As the surgery had been planned, so had the coverage. So, whoever Dr Bannerman really was, she'd just need to hope for the best. All she really needed him to do was give her a green tick.

As she did every morning, she bypassed her office—stopping only to throw in her laptop and bag—and headed to the nurses' station in the oncology ward. It was the heart of their department—and where she could find out everything she needed to know. Indira, the ward sister, was doing a handover to all staff—allocating patients, making sure all tests would be followed up. She ran a tight ship. Skye loved working with her, and the rest of the staff in this ward. There was a real team spirit.

Connie, the ward receptionist, appeared with a large tray of biscuits, a wide smile on her face. The rest of the staff gave a little cheer and helped themselves. Skye listened to the rest of the handover, making a few mental notes of things to follow up.

One of the nurses handed over a firm envelope addressed to her. The writing on the envelope was beautiful, and as Skye opened and pulled out the cream card, her face broke into a wide smile, a warm feeling spreading inside her.

'It's an invite,' she said, 'to Fiona and Armando's wedding.' Fiona was a patient they'd treated over the last eighteen months, who'd finally managed to ring the bell that signalled the end of her treatment.

'That's fantastic,' said Lleyton, the ward physio. 'Didn't they have to postpone initially because she was so sick?'

Skye nodded. 'They did. But Fiona finally gets to have her special day.' She hugged the card close to her chest. She'd sat next to Fiona whilst she'd sobbed during her treatments, and when she'd felt so sick. Seeing her out the other side was a delight. And it reinforced the hope she had for all her patients—that good things can happen, and life can get better.

A moment later she was distracted by the sight of a dark-suited man striding down the corridor towards them. She didn't recognise him, but they often had visiting staff in the Great Northern.

Connie turned and held out the biscuit tray towards him. He didn't even acknowledge her. Just kept walking, coming to a sharp halt and glaring at the white fairy lights strung from underneath the nurse's station to the tops of the walls.

His gaze stopped dead on Skye. She had no idea who he was, but he better change his attitude fast. No one got to ignore Connie. Not on her watch.

She met his glare as she pointedly leaned forward to lift one of the delicious smelling biscuits.

'Thank you, Connie,' she said, smiling at Connie, but still side-eyeing the gentleman in the hope he would get the not-so-secret message.

He did get the message, looking her clearly in the eye. 'I'm here to meet Dr Campbell, not eat sweets.'

There was an instant chill across her skin. That Irish accent. It sent shockwaves through her system, making her catch her breath. There was only one person who would be looking for her that she didn't know. But she hadn't expected him here for another few days. Wasn't he moving up from London? How could he have got here so quickly?

And why did he have to look like that? Tall, with dark wavy hair, penetrating brown eyes and a lean body. He should be a leading man in some Hollywood rom-com.

In a wave of panic, she hoped her gaze hadn't been obvious. Because she knew exactly how she wanted to come across to this man. It was clear he had no idea who she was, because he started to glance around, as if he expected Dr Campbell to appear out of thin air.

Skye took a quick glance down at her out-
fit. She wasn't wearing her white coat, but was
dressed in a long-sleeved, mid-length pink pat-
terned dress, with buttons down the front and
tied at the waist. It was a favourite.

'I'm Dr Campbell,' she said, knowing that all
eyes were on them. 'Follow me to my office.'

She didn't wait. She walked back down the
corridor, opening her office door and waiting
as he came inside. Her nerves were jangling.
She needed this guy to be on board with her
research project, she really didn't want to get
off on the wrong foot—but it seemed that Dr
Grumpy might not extend her the same courtesy.

She closed the door firmly and walked around
her desk, sitting down and placing her arms on
the desk. She leaned a little towards him.

'Can I assume that you are Jay Bannerman?'

He gave the briefest nod, so she started talking. Better just to take the bull by the horns.

'Dr Bannerman, we are a team around here. A
team that works well together. I don't want anything to disrupt my team. And a few moments
ago? That was downright rude.'

His body gave a little jerk and he straightened
up. 'Excuse me?'

'I'll just put my cards on the table.' She was
careful with her tone, mindful that she knew

nothing about this man, or his background. She tried to give him a smile. 'No one is rude to Connie, not on my watch.'

'Excuse me?' he repeated. He kind of looked like a deer caught in headlights. His reputation as Dr Grumpy had travelled from one hospital to another. Had no one ever spoken to this guy about his manner?

She took a breath. 'Connie is our receptionist. She's been here since the hospital was built.' Skye paused for a second. What she was going to reveal was generally known by everyone who worked here, but it felt like breaking a confidence.

'Connie has had a really hard life. She was a victim of domestic abuse for years. It took her a while before she could tell someone and make plans to leave. Her grown-up daughter has alcohol issues. Connie deals with all this on her own. When Connie gets stressed,' Skye gave a wave of her hand, 'she bakes.'

His shoulders relaxed just a touch, as if he was beginning to understand where she was going with this.

'So,' Skye continued, 'when Connie appears with tins of biscuits, or traybakes or loafs, we know. We know something is going on with her, and that she needs some support.' Skye licked her lips and met those brown eyes. 'That's why I'll never let anyone be rude to Connie on my watch, and...' she paused '... I hope you won't either.'

'I'm not a social worker.'

Skye bristled, but her words stayed calm. 'I'm not asking you to be a social worker, Dr Bannerman. I'm asking you to be kind and considerate to your colleagues.' Then she just couldn't help herself. 'But with your length of time in the job, I really shouldn't have to.'

There was a long silence. She hoped she'd handled this the way she should have. Tone was everything—Skye knew that. She hadn't spoken angrily, or accusingly. She hoped everything she'd said had come across as kindly as possible.

This guy didn't know her background. He didn't know why she was here. For Skye, cancer research was personal. And she didn't know his background, what had made him do years of training and decide that oncology was the place he wanted to work. She wasn't here to make an enemy. But from the expression on his face, she was doubting she was making a friend.

She decided to push in another direction. 'You know,' she said breezily, 'I am a huge Christmas fan. You'll learn that over the next few weeks.

My favourite movie is *The Grinch*. I'd hate for people to start calling you that.'

The edges of his mouth hinted upwards and he gave a sigh, as his eyebrows raised. The expression had the hint of a cheeky teenager about it. 'My nickname is Dr Grumpy, and yes, I know that,' he replied in that delicious, thick Irish accent.

'And mine is Miss Sunshine,' she replied, holding her hand out to his.

Jay Bannerman didn't even hide his groan as he shook her hand. 'This is going to be a disaster, isn't it?'

For a second—at least in Skye's head—things froze. She was captured by the man sitting in front of her. Now she'd stopped focusing on everything else, she realised just how handsome he was. Discounting the fact that every time he spoke with his lilting accent, which sent a whole host of vibrations down her spine, even if he hadn't opened his mouth, and she'd seen him in a bar, this guy was hot.

Skye didn't mix business with pleasure. She'd never been interested in dating her colleagues.

But at least he was semi-smiling now, and she would take that. He stood up and straightened his suit jacket. 'Let me go back and make a better impression on our staff, then you can show

me where my office is, and hopefully point me
in the direction of where to pick up my laptop.
We need to talk about your research project.'

She felt a tiny chill on her skin. 'Of course.'
She didn't like the way her voice sounded.

He gave her the briefest of glances and then
walked to the door. Jay didn't waste any time—
he walked back down the corridor to where Connie was sitting behind the nurses' station. The
tray of biscuits was sitting above her.

Jay walked around beside her and held out his
hand. 'Hi, Connie? I'm Jay Bannerman. I'm an
oncologist from the Great Southern and I'm up
here with special privileges to see patients, and
to oversee Dr Campbell's research project. We'll
be working together.'

Since Skye had been on his heels she'd heard
every word. It appeared that Jay could turn on
the charm when he chose to, and his Irish accent was almost therapeutic. If Connie was
surprised, she hid it well, and shook his out-
stretched hand.

She didn't get a chance to respond, as Jay
lifted his other hand to grab a biscuit. 'And I
have it on good authority that you're a wonderful baker, so thanks for the biscuit.'

It wasn't an apology as such. But at least he
was making an effort.

Connie gave a cautious nod. 'If you need any assistance with anything just let me know, Dr Bannerman. I'm happy to help.'

He gave a nod. 'Dr Campbell's just about to get me set up with a laptop. I'll let you know if I need anything.'

Connie gave a nervous glance and handed Skye a slip of paper. 'You've just had a call about an emergency admission. GP is sending them straight up as he doesn't want the patient going through A&E.' Connie was very switched on and knew exactly what that meant. 'Why don't you go and call him and I'll get Dr Bannerman his ID, show him his office and get his laptop set up?'

Skye took the piece of paper and read it quickly. 'Sorry, Jay,' she said automatically, 'I'll have to prioritise this patient.'

His brown eyes met hers for a moment. She couldn't quite make out that expression. Calculating? He gave a small nod. 'Since I have privileges, I'd like to see how things work. Why don't you give me a shout when the patient arrives so I can familiarise myself with all the processes? I'm sure I'll be in good hands with Connie up until then.'

She wanted to say no. She wanted to refuse to let him oversee her. She didn't need him for that. The only thing he was supposed to do was oversee her research project. But that was making her oddly nervous too. She glanced down at the name on the paper. Leah McLeod—a teenage girl. That's where her focus had to be.

Not on this doctor. Or what he thought of her. Or her project.

She fixed a smile to her face. 'No problem at all. Thanks Connie, I'll give you a shout when our patient arrives.'

And she walked quickly back to her office, phoned the GP and organised some tests for Leah's arrival.

Jay Bannerman wasn't quite sure if this was a good day or a bad day.

He hadn't exactly made the impression he'd wanted to. But then again, he didn't spend much of his life worrying about what people thought of him.

But the truth was—he wasn't happy to be here, and he was having trouble putting a 'face' on. Yet another trick he'd never really mastered.

He'd worked at the Great Southern in London for ten years. Five of those years he'd been engaged to Jessica Morris, a fellow doctor. They'd agreed on a long engagement, not wanting to rush into marriage. But a year ago she'd broken things off, saying she wasn't ready.

Now, she apparently was ready. But not for marriage to him. She'd just announced her surprise engagement to one of their colleagues— Peter Benson. And Jay really didn't want to stay around and witness the fun.

He knew he had a bit of reputation for being serious and introverted. But since his break-up with Jess, he'd definitely got worse. As far as he was concerned, his patient care was still excellent, but he was reluctant to form any new friendships here in Scotland. He didn't want any romantic entanglements with colleagues. He didn't really want people knowing his business. The truth was, when it came to personal relationships now, he wasn't sure he could trust his own judgement.

So, the fact that the person he was directly supervising looked as gorgeous as a movie star, and could clearly hold her own, was making every part of his body groan. Skye Campbell had dark curly hair that had been pulled back from her face, with surprisingly dark green eyes. Her pink dress suited her, it covered up every part of her, but still managed to show off her curves. Something he absolutely shouldn't have noticed, or be focusing on.

His nickname of Dr Grumpy had clearly been no surprise to her. But, somehow, he knew it wasn't his rudeness that had rattled her. He sensed something more. It was almost as if she were wary of him.

And she should be. He was there to assess her work, and to investigate any potential controversies over the use of artificial intelligence in the prediction of cancer growth rates. As with all research projects, it had gone through countless committees before approval and funding. But he still had a number of valid questions he needed to raise with her.

'Dr Bannerman?'

He looked up from the desk. Connie had escorted him to HR, security and then IT. He now had an ID badge and security pass, white coat, his emails transferred and his laptop set up. Connie was just linking him to a few hospital systems specific to their ward now.

She took a few moments to show him where to access test results and how to order bloods, X-rays, ECGs and a whole range of other tests— all things that happened on a daily basis in the oncology unit.

She showed him where the research study data was stored, and how to access patient records. Connie was exceedingly good at her job.

'I don't think I've missed anything, but if you think of something, just let me know.'

She pulled up the ward details and nodded at the admission list. 'Looks like Leah McLeod has arrived.' She turned the laptop around to Jay and pointed at the young woman's name. 'If you click here, you'll be able to pull up her records.'

Jay sat back and nodded. 'Thanks very much, Connie, you've been a big help.' He shot her the best smile he could. 'It's much appreciated.'

He could see the expression on Connie's face, and the slight relaxation of her shoulders. He got it. He got why Skye was protective over her colleague. There were good intentions here, and he would be more mindful in future.

He scanned Leah's records and the brief notes from the GP that had referred her. Leah had presented at the surgery with some classic signs, and the GP had taken some bloods before he'd sent her to hospital. Jay could see the blood results now.

He gave a nod and stood up, asking Connie which bed, and heading to the side room where he knew Skye would already be. He wondered if she would have told him Leah was here or just ploughed on without him. But as he reached the door, she gave him a smile and waved him in.

'Leah, this is Dr Bannerman, the other doctor I said would see you too.'

Leah was as pale as the hospital bedsheets. Her father—an extremely anxious looking man—was standing against a wall. He looked like he might be sick.

Jay walked over and put a hand on his arm. 'Mr McLeod? I'm Jay Bannerman. Let me assure you that we're going to look after your daughter.'

Skye positioned herself next to the bed, glancing at Jay. 'I've got the notes from your GP, and I spoke to him earlier when you were on the way up. He told me you had a UTI last week, and it looks like you've a chest infection this week. You've noticed some bruising. You had a couple of knocks recently and it's been difficult to control the bleeding.'

Leah gave an anxious nod. 'I play hockey. At least I did until last week. But this week I just couldn't breathe.'

She pulled back the covers to show Skye the top of her leg. 'I clashed with someone else. I've never bruised like this before.'

The angry bruise was still red and purple. A week-old bruise would normally have faded slightly, and the edge turned yellow. There were also plasters on her knees.

Jay moved to the other side of the bed. 'Did you skin your knees at the same time?'

Leah nodded and frowned. 'But they just keep bleeding. They haven't even scabbed yet.' She looked down at the inside of her elbow, where a cotton wool ball was held in place with some tape. 'Even where Dr Gillespie took blood—it's still bleeding.'

Skye lifted her stethoscope from around her neck. 'If it's okay, I'd like to listen to your chest. If we think you have a chest infection, we'll start you on antibiotics right away.'

Leah leaned forward and Skye gave her instructions to breathe in and out slowly, before moving her stethoscope around to the front and nodding as she listened.

She looked over to Jay and Leah's father. 'I'm going to pull the curtains for a second, just to check Leah's lymph nodes.'

Jay helped tug the curtain around. Leah's dad looked a bit confused. 'There's lymph nodes at your neck, under your arms and in your groin area,' he explained. 'Because your daughter's a teenage girl, we try to give some privacy.'

He nodded, still looking overwhelmed by everything. 'My wife's away on a business trip in Germany. She says she'll get the first flight back she can.' He shook his head and blinked back tears. 'As soon as the doctor said he was sending us up to the oncology ward...' His words tailed off.

Skye pulled the curtains back. 'So, Leah's lymph nodes are swollen.'

'What does that mean?' asked Leah. 'Why is everyone so worried? And why do I feel so rubbish?'

Skye gave him the briefest look. She was doing a great job. He was impressed. And he wanted to be clear they were a team.

He sat down next to Leah. 'We'll need to run a few more tests. But from your symptoms, and your initial blood tests, we think you could have a condition called acute lymphoblastic leukaemia. The only way we can get a definite diagnosis is if we do something called a bone marrow biopsy. And we'd like to do that tonight if we can.' He watched Leah carefully. 'Your dad says your mum is coming back. If your mum can get a flight today, we can wait until she's here to do the next test. Dr Campbell and I are happy to wait.'

Skye reached over and squeezed Leah's hand. 'I'll explain everything about the test to you. Don't worry.'

'Leukaemia is cancer.' Leah blinked.

Skye nodded and kept her hand over Leah's.

'It is. It's a cancer of the blood. And we have lots of ways to treat it. We can talk all that over too.' She looked over at Mr McLeod. 'Would you be able to find out if your wife has managed to get a flight tonight? And is there anyone else you would like to call?'

Mr McLeod looked like a deer caught in headlights.

Jay put an arm behind him, guiding him to the door. 'Leah, why don't you write a list of everything you want your dad to bring from home? It's likely you'll need to stay with us for a few days. So, comfy clothes, a tablet if you have one, any toiletries you want, books?'

Skye pulled a tiny notepad from the pocket of her satin dress and handed it over. 'Favourite sweets,' she said with a smile. 'That's what I always tell people to put first on their list.'

'Am I going to lose my little girl?' asked Mr McLeod as soon as they stepped outside.

The door was still open and Jay could see Skye talking to Leah and keeping her occupied. He was always honest with his patients and their relatives and he hated this part. But this was him, this was his job. 'I certainly hope not. The odds are in her favour. She's fifteen—the younger the diagnosis, the better the chances. Overall, we look at the five-year survival rate

and for this disease it's around sixty-five per-
cent. Lots of things affect this, and I'll talk to
you about it all. But first, let's get her chest
infection sorted and her bone marrow biopsy
done. We have lots of treatments, and it all depends on how Leah reacts to them. If one kind
of treatment doesn't work as well as we hoped,
we have other options. We also have some clin-
ical trials. Honestly?' He looked Mr McLeod
in the eye. 'Your daughter is in one of the best
hospitals. And we'll be with you every step of
the way.'

For a moment Jay honestly thought the man in
front of him was going to collapse. There was no
one else around them. He could hear quiet voices
in the unit. After a few seconds he saw a wave of
a hand at the bottom of the corridor. It was one
of the healthcare support workers dressed in a
grey tunic. The staff member pointed to a chair
in a kind of query, and Jay gave a small nod,
as the guy quickly retrieved one and brought it
along the corridor to them.

The healthcare support worker was an older
man, built as if he did weights. He slid the chair
next to Mr McLeod and put a hand on his shoulder. 'What can I get you? Tea? Coffee, or something sweet to drink?'

'Coffee,' said Mr McLeod automatically, his

legs folding beneath him as he collapsed onto the seat. 'Thank you,' it came out absentmindedly as his phone beeped.

He looked up at Jay. 'I almost didn't take her to the GP. My wife usually takes care of that kind of stuff. But her colour—she was just so pale. And she'd felt off for the last few days. We just couldn't really put our finger on anything but...' His voice tailed again and Jay lowered himself so he would be at eye level with Mr McLeod.

'Onset can be really rapid. You did the right thing.' He took a breath as he let the man collect himself a bit. 'Your phone—was that your wife?'

He looked surprised for a moment, then pulled the phone from his pocket. Jay could see how relief swamped his body. 'She got on standby at Berlin airport and someone gave up their seat for her.' His voice broke a little. 'How nice is that?'

Jay gave a smile. 'People can surprise you sometimes.'

He was conscious of Skye and Leah still in the side room. He could tell that Skye was having a serious conversation with Leah, and was holding her hand as she spoke to her. He could only hear a few words, but Skye was encouraging Leah to ask questions.

Mr McLeod took a deep breath. 'Her flight takes off in forty-five minutes. She lands at five o'clock and will come straight here.'

Jay gave him a smile. 'That's great news.' He looked up as the healthcare support worker approached, carrying a tray with two steaming cups and a plate of chocolate biscuits—and some of Connie's cookies.

'Why don't I take this into Leah's room? Hot chocolate for her, and coffee for you.'

The healthcare worker headed in and put the tray down on the table next to Leah, who immediately looked up in surprise. Skye took her cue to leave, to let dad and daughter talk to each other, and walked out to join Jay again.

He was impressed by how seamlessly the team did things around here. The ward had a calm atmosphere, and the staff seemed to anticipate the needs of the patients well.

'Who is the healthcare assistant?'

'That's Ronnie, he's our gentle giant, but also our security guard when required.'

'You have trouble on the ward?' Jay was surprised by this.

'Emotions are always heightened on an oncology ward.' She gave a sad smile. 'Either it's warring sons and daughters over their mum or dad, or divorced parents over a child.' She gestured her hand down to the fairy lights on the desk. 'And whilst I love Christmas, for some families it's a hard time of year.'

She licked her lips for a second and gave him a careful stare. It was hard not to be captivated by those dark green eyes. But his heart had already sunk a little. He generally knew what a look like that meant.

'Dr Bannerman,' she said quietly.

'Yes?' He kept his face straight. He wasn't going to show any sign of weakness.

'I appreciate you have a great deal of knowledge in treating cancers. But…' she glanced over her shoulder, back to the room where Leah and her dad were '… I'm not sure Mr McLeod was ready for news like that.'

'I'm not sure he was either. But he asked me a direct question. I don't lie to my patients or their relatives, Dr Campbell.' If she wanted to be formal, so could he.

He'd already seen her in action with Leah. She was one of these people who had a natural rapport with others, who could engage at their level and be their friend.

'I'm their doctor,' he reiterated. 'Not their friend.'

Skye pulled something slightly bent from the

pocket of her dress. 'But sometimes we can be both,' she said easily.

He could see from first glance it was a wedding invitation.

She held it up. 'This is from a patient we all treated for the last eighteen months. I find it impossible not to form therapeutic relationships with my patients.'

And he could already see that. He'd love to be that kind of doctor, but that had always been a struggle for him.

She bowed her head a little, though it wasn't in any way deferential. She was obviously finding a way to say something. She lifted her head again and met his gaze. 'We'll find a way to work together well. I would have waited until Mrs McLeod was here to do the biopsy and give the news to the family together, but that's too late now. Perhaps,' she licked those lips again, and Jay tried to focus on something else, 'in future, we could have a chat about breaking bad news and maybe I could do that part?' She gave a wary smile. 'You could do the part about what type of treatment you recommend, since that's your area of expertise?'

She framed it as a question, but he wasn't naïve enough to know that this woman had just told him how this should go.

'I'll consider it.' He tried not to outwardly bristle.

Her face broke into a wide smile. 'Good,' she said, then gave him a cheeky wink as she started down the corridor. 'And here was you thinking this was going to be a disaster.'

CHAPTER TWO

THE NEXT WEEK was slightly odd. Skye concentrated on her patients, trying to find a way to work well with Jay Bannerman. He hadn't really revealed much of his character, and seemed so guarded at times. Skye had never been one for gossip, but had made a few casual enquiries with colleagues at the Great Southern. She'd learned that his previous fiancée had just announced her engagement to another doctor. Was that why he had come up here?

She would have loved it if she'd thought that Jay Bannerman had wanted to come up here to supervise her meticulous research project. But, so far, he'd barely mentioned it to her, with the exception of requesting a few files.

Leah McLeod's mother had arrived on the day she'd been admitted to the ward. She was with her daughter whilst she had her bone marrow biopsy, which had confirmed the diagnosis she and Jay had suspected. Her chest infection had taken hold, and she'd had a few days of intravenous antibiotics, before they'd even had the conversation around treatment and the fact it could cause immunosuppression. She'd then been allowed a day at home, before coming back in to start her treatment regime.

Leah's mother had been a steadying force on both her husband and daughter. She was a business woman—she was used to being in control. But both Skye and Jay had caught her crying at moments, and taken her out of the ward to talk to her and let her gather herself. Skye knew just how overwhelming the first few weeks could be, and wanted to ensure she supported the whole family the best way she could. She didn't need to worry about the rest of the staff. They knew exactly what was needed for newly diagnosed patients and their families, and she trusted them. This was the good thing about working in a ward with people she knew well.

The hospital had started to play Christmas music, and people were starting to complain that it was only the third week in November. But Skye would happily play Christmas music all year round. She reached the nurses' station that morning and plunked down a Christmas container. One of the staff picked it up and looked through the plastic edges suspiciously. 'What is this?'

'Christmas chocolate tiffin. Made by my own fair hands.' She was laughing already as they all knew she wasn't entirely skilled in the baking department. 'It's a tray bake,' she added. 'Nearly impossible to burn.'

Her colleague lifted up the edge of the container and sniffed. 'Smells okay. It might be edible.'

'I'll have you know that I nearly offered Max Robertson a bit in the lift this morning, in order to try and coax a smile out of him.'

Lleyton, the physio, laughed. 'If it's anything like your sultana muffins, it wouldn't have got you a smile.'

'You're being mean now,' she shot back.

'Only to you. But honestly, what's it going to take to get that guy to crack a smile. They're actually taking bets on it now.'

Skye frowned. 'Who?'

'All the other wards.'

She waved her hand. 'No, that's definitely mean. He's good with his patients, the kids love him and, apparently, he helps out at a local children's home. Maybe he just uses up all his smiles there?'

The rest of them groaned and Lleyton leaned

forward. 'Maybe we should take bets on our own guy. He's a bit serious too, isn't he?'

And this is why she tried not to get involved in hospital gossip. Because it really wouldn't do if her research supervisor came out here and caught her talking about him.

'Leave me out of it,' she said breezily as she headed down to her office.

She had work to do, patients to see. The unit had been even busier than usual. As well as her research work, she'd been covering extra duties since one of her colleagues was on maternity leave. But Skye didn't mind. Returning to an empty home at night wasn't always the best thing in the world. She knew she was lucky to be able to afford her own place to live, but since she didn't have a partner or a flatmate, the place sometimes seemed a little hollow. And Skye still didn't like too much time on her hands. It gave her too much time to think.

To think about her father, and how treatments had potentially changed, and how he might have had a better outcome if he were diagnosed now instead of then.

She'd contemplated getting a cat. She thought she was likely more of a dog person, but the hours she worked weren't conducive to owning a dog, so a cat was a definite possibility.

'Dr Campbell?' The unexpected Irish voice caught her by surprise. She thought he'd gone home already.

'Jay? What are you still doing here? And call me Skye. Dr Campbell makes me feel old.'

He glanced over his shoulder. 'I don't like to be overly familiar in front of patients.'

She held up her arms in her empty office. 'See any patients?'

He gave a sigh and came in and sat down. 'We haven't really had a chance to talk about your research project. I've read the documents you sent, and wondered if you had some time to discuss it?'

Her stomach gave a nervous flip. She'd actually prepared for this conversation virtually every day since last week, but as he hadn't approached her she'd sort of relaxed about it. Now it felt like he'd caught her on the hop.

But…he was still the person to oversee her research, so she painted an appropriate smile on her face and gestured to the chair on the other side of her desk. 'Of course.'

How weird. To get any research proposal off the ground, the proposer had to sit through countless research committees, both in hospitals and at universities, often being grilled within an inch of their life. Skye had done this on more than one occasion. She'd always been passionate about her work, and had researched things fastidiously. So, she should be confident about this. But Jay Bannerman was having an unnerving effect on her—and she wasn't quite sure why.

'Where would you like to start?' He leaned back in the chair. He'd taken off his white coat and was wearing a mid-blue short-sleeved shirt and navy trousers. He had a bit of a rumpled look about him. A bit like that TV doc in the show set in Seattle.

The question he'd just asked rattled around her brain. She knew exactly where she would start in front of an ethics committee. But she'd done all that. She didn't want to do those practised spiels again.

Maybe it was the long day she'd just had. Maybe it was the fact she hadn't quite got the measure of Jay Bannerman yet. Maybe she was just a little tired. So, she did what she did when talking to friend. She spoke from the heart.

'The unofficial name of the project—and the name I always use when talking about it, is the Hope Project.'

She blew a few strands of hair out of her eyes. 'My dad died of cancer when I was doing my medical training. It immediately changed my course as a doctor. It was clear I didn't understand cancer, but I did have experience of what a cancer diagnosis did to a family. I understood the ripple effect better than anyone, and I realised that the tiny spider web wasn't just the picture of what a cancer cell could do in a body, it was also the impact of cancer on everything surrounding the person. Their family, their relationships, their job or their ability to work, their insurance, or lack of chance of getting any. The impact of the treatment, the changes to their everyday living. Sometimes changes in their appearance. The hopes and dreams that they lost, along with their family members or friends who were on that journey with them.'

She sighed and sat back, fixing her eyes on the wall instead of Jay. She knew his gaze was fixed on her, but she didn't want to lose focus now she was in full flow.

'What's the one question every patient diagnosed with cancer asks? What's the question every parent asks? Once they think there can't be a complete cure, they ask about time. All of them. Everyone. I can't remember a patient in that position who hasn't asked me. And what do we tell them? Our best guess. Sometimes we are right, and sometimes we are wrong. And when we're wrong, we hate ourselves. Even though we try to reason with ourselves about it.' She took a deep breath. 'So, time. That's essentially what's at the heart of this project.'

He leaned forward on the desk, pulling her attention. A frown creased his brow. 'Do you honestly think that telling someone how much time they have left is really a good thing?'

She held out both hands. 'For some patients? Yes. But not for all. That's where we come in. That's where we will know our patients well enough to understand whether they can deal with news like that. Artificial intelligence can help us predict how cancers will evolve and spread. It can pick out patterns in DNA mutations and use that information to forecast future genetic changes. We will know if a tumour is likely to become drug resistant and change treatments accordingly. We'll be able to predict cancer's next move, and eventually its lifecycle. There's been some earlier work of this nature done in breast cancer, and now it's time to look at cancers of the lung, bowel, liver and kidney.'

'And artificial intelligence is really the way forward to do this?' He ran his fingers through his hair.

She tilted her head to one side. 'You have something against artificial intelligence?'

He gave a small shrug. 'My sister is a writer as well as being a university lecturer. She has lots to say about artificial intelligence—particularly around the amount of fake essays it generates, and the amount of fake books that haven't been written by real people.'

Skye raised her eyebrows. 'And your sister would be right. But this is different. This is just the latest version of our technology. Don't you remember the pictures of the NASA mathematicians standing next to their huge stacks of paper—Katherine Johnson—when they made the calculations to get to the moon? Don't you remember that computers used to fill a whole room?' She held up her phone. 'Or the fact that our modern smart phones have more technology than the guidance system Apollo Eleven used?'

He gave a small smile. 'You like your space trivia.'

'I'm just fascinated that I live in a world where technology seems to be progressing at a tremendous rate. And whilst some students want to use it to cheat on their essays, I want to use it help our patients, and help find some of the answers that cancer has hidden from us for years.'

He tapped his fingers on the table for a moment. 'I read a book recently, where people could find out how long they would live.' He shook his head. 'It really didn't work out well for most of them.'

She met his gaze. Those brown eyes were really something, but they wouldn't dissuade her. 'My dad's cancer progressed extremely quickly. We thought we'd have more time. If I'd known,' she put her hand on her heart, 'I would have taken a year off university and spent it all with him.'

Jay didn't speak, just watched her carefully.

'I absolutely expect your area of interest to be around the tracking of the mutations,' she continued, 'identifying repeating patterns and predicting the future trajectory of tumour development, and how different treatments can impact on that. I fully expect we could work on this for the next twenty years. Maybe it will revolutionise how we treat certain cancers.'

She paused again. 'But time—the bit that no one really wants to talk about, and pays the least attention to? That's the bit of information I wanted when I was eighteen years old. And I'll never forget that.'

Jay was trying to take everything in. This was the heart of the project for her. And she was right. It fundamentally was the least important part, because the prediction for how a certain tumour might grow, and to know how to treat that most effectively, was the part that the majority of the world would consider the key aspects. They certainly were for him.

But all of a sudden he was glad he'd had this conversation. He'd read her proposals. And this part had been hidden in amongst everything else. He would never have found out her family history, or the impact it'd had on her world.

He was struck how much she'd gone through at such a crucial point in her life.

Her hair had released itself from the clasp at the back of her head as she'd spoken, and now her dark curls were sitting on her shoulders. The green dress she wore reflected her dark green eyes, enhancing their colour. It was almost like Skye Campbell had just unwrapped herself in front of him, and he couldn't imagine how vulnerable that might make her feel.

If this was his history, would he have been able to tell her the same?

Every cell in his body cringed at the mere thought. Since his love life had previously been the business of everyone in the Southern, he'd spent the last year wanting to live his life in a private bubble. Revealing any part of himself might make him open to being hurt again. It was a road he just didn't want to take.

'So, you qualified as a doctor, then did a research doctorate?'

Skye smiled and shook her head, sliding open a drawer in her desk and bringing out a large box of chocolates. 'I'm essentially a glutton for punishment.'

He bit his lip. 'What kind of doctor might you have been?'

He asked the question just as she bit into a chocolate and pushed the box towards him.

'What?' As she asked the question some gooey caramel dripped down her chin. She made an elaborate mission of trying to catch it, and failed miserably.

He laughed, then repeated, 'If that hadn't happened to your dad, what kind of direction do you think you might have taken?'

She grabbed a tissue and wiped her chin, biting the inside of her cheek as she contemplated the question. 'No one has actually asked me that before,' she admitted.

'Really?'

'Really.' She sat back and licked her lips of caramel. She sighed. 'If you want absolute honesty, I was thinking medicine wasn't for me. I fancied myself as a Lara Croft type and wanted to switch to archaeology.'

'No way.' The words were out before he had time to think.

'Maybe I just wanted to wear an Indiana Jones type fedora?'

'You would have changed your course?'

She nodded. 'I was young and naïve. The first year of medical school is dull. You know that.' He raised his eyebrows and she laughed. 'Go on admit it. The only thing good about first year is telling people you're going to be a doctor. The actual study part is hideous.'

He'd never thought about it that way, and now he actually laughed. 'You could be right. I never loved the biochemistry.'

Her face lit up and she leaned towards him. 'I *hated* it. But when dad got sick my whole world just turned. I became extra focused. I wanted to learn about cancer. I was interested in the cellular level, the pathology, the journey. Every aspect of it drove me on. I never even considered any other speciality. It was always oncology. There was no other option for me.'

'That's interesting,' he said. She had leaned towards him, and now he could see her face in much more detail. She had tiny lines around her eyes, smiling lines or laughter lines from what little he knew of her. Those dark green eyes were something, and her dark curls framing her face. She had tiny freckles over her nose, but her skin was pale. He found himself wondering if she got a tan in the summer.

The aroma of her perfume was drifting towards him. Hints of amber and spice. It suited her. And it made him want to lean closer.

'Why is that interesting?' she asked, and her voice brought him back to the topic sharply.

He gave a wry kind of laugh and sat backwards, leaning into his chair. It seemed the right thing to do, even though he was reluctant to move away from her.

He didn't tell people much about himself. But she'd revealed a piece of herself that was almost at an intimate level. And it was he who had directed this conversation. It was only fair.

He slipped up his sleeve, revealing a white disc on his outer arm.

'You're diabetic?' She recognised the device immediately. It was fairly common place now.

He nodded. 'Since I was eight. I had measles, and went on to develop Type One. I was pretty good as a teenager, didn't stop taking insulin, no crazy diets, no drinking binges. I had a great diabetic nurse who also wrote a reference for my university application. But from the second I started medical school I knew what area I *wasn't* going to study.'

Her eyes widened, and she seemed fascinated.

'Really? But why? Don't you want to know everything?'

He gave a slow nod. 'I do. But I live with diabetes every day. I realised quickly I didn't want to work with it every day too.'

He could see the recognition of those words hitting home with her. She was clearly thinking back to her own training.

He held out his hands. 'I know I'm at higher risk for basically everything. I have this sensor,' he patted his arm, 'I get an annual review, my bloods are checked, my eyes and feet are checked. I'm lucky. I haven't had any major problems.'

'But as long as you look after yourself, you shouldn't have.'

He pulled a face. 'That's kind of an idealistic view.'

'You think?'

'Well, what do you think your risk of cancer is? Some studies say that one in every two people will develop some form of cancer.'

She nodded. 'We know that some cancers have genetic components, we know that some have contributory lifestyle factors, others environmental, and some are just bad luck. So, I guess I have the same chance as everyone else.'

He liked how she was willing to have these

kinds of conversations. It gave him a good sense of her. This had started off being about her research project, and had taken them both down another path.

'Okay,' he said, 'so, from my perspective, if I'd specialised in diabetes, I would have seen all the problem patients. The ones with end-stage issues. The patients with renal failure that require dialysis. The teenagers who don't accept their condition and come in and out in ketoacidosis, who play with their life, not realising how close to death they come, or the long-term damage they do to every part of their body.'

She took a deep breath. 'Okay,' she said. 'But devil's advocate?'

Jeez, he actually liked this woman more and more every minute. She was intelligent, insightful and also really, really easy to talk to. Jay couldn't remember the last time he'd had a conversation like this.

He gave a soft shoulder shrug. 'Go on.'

She actually laughed. 'Please say that again.'

'What?'

'Those words, the go on. With your accent it's just…' She didn't finish the sentence.

He gave a smile. 'Go on then.'

She gave a shiver and a broad smile that made tiny hairs on his body stand on end.

'Okay,' she shook her head, 'I'll get back to where we should be.' She swallowed and continued, her fingers going to her throat, toying with the gold pendant around her neck. 'Think of studies you could have got involved in—all around those sensors,' she pointed to his arm, 'or new insulins, the pumps or even the beta cell implant work.'

He sighed. 'I read the studies. I keep up to date. But I don't want diabetes to consume every minute of every day for me.' He licked his lips and leaned forward, keeping his voice low. 'Because the reality is, it already does.'

His gaze connected with hers, and again he saw some recognition. She stopped leaning on the desk and sat back herself.

'Wow,' she said.

He took a deep breath. 'Maybe this just proves what we already know?'

She frowned. 'And what's that?'

'You said you're Miss Sunshine here, and I'm,' he pulled a face and raised his eyebrows, 'Dr Grumpy, or Grinch, since it's coming up to Christmas.'

Her smile broadened. 'But what does that mean?'

'We're opposites,' he said decisively. 'You saw cancer in your family and jumped in, immersed yourself in everything about it, to take part in both caring for patients and studies. You've actively pursued everything around it.' He gave another shrug. 'I was diagnosed diabetic as a child, and whilst I look after myself, I've purposely chosen to walk in a different direction. I don't want to immerse myself in it. I want my work to be about something else.'

She leaned an elbow on the desk and put her face in her hand. 'I'm not sure we're opposites,' she said in a complacent tone. '*I* wasn't affected by cancer. If it was me, I might have felt entirely differently.'

'You might,' he agreed, 'and I might have felt differently if my sister had been the one diagnosed with diabetes, and had issues that I would've wanted to assist with.'

'Jelly babies?' she asked out the blue.

'What?' He shook his head in confusion.

'Other diabetics I know keep jelly babies around them in case they go low. Is that what you eat?' She gave him a cheeky wink. 'I need to know if I should buy a bag to keep in my drawer.'

He shuddered. 'I absolutely hate jelly babies.' He paused and looked at her. 'Digestive biscuits. That's what I like. Chocolate digestives even more.'

'Don't they take too long to be absorbed and work?'

'We're all individuals. They seem to work for me.' He tapped his arm. 'My alarm usually gives me plenty warning. It's not as if I'm a surgeon and on my feet for twelve hours at a time, or have people's lives in my hands. If I alarm, I have a seat for five minutes, eat a biscuit and give it time to kick in. I never get so low that I'm irritated or incoherent.'

She tilted her head to the side. 'You must have as a child. Alarms didn't exist then.'

He smiled and nodded. 'My mother spent her life at the side of football or rugby pitches with an array of things in her pockets. But I did have hypo warning signs, so I always knew if I needed to come off.' He raised his eyebrows. 'I didn't always want to come off. At times I ran past with my hand held out for her to stuff something into it.'

'I bet she loved that.'

He kept grinning. 'I had to be quick in case she made a grab for me. But I was speedy back then.'

Her eyes ran over his frame—it gave him a tingle that she was obviously sizing him up.

'You still look speedy,' she said simply.

'I run,' he said, wondering if this was verging on flirtation. Tiny red flags started waving in his brain, but he ignored them.

'I don't,' she replied so swiftly he laughed out loud.

He let his eyes take in her curves underneath her dress. 'You look just as speedy yourself,' he said, following her backward compliment.

'I would like to say that I walk my dog, but I don't have one.'

He looked at her curiously. 'You want one.'

'I've contemplated one for the last three years. But I think it's going to be a cat for me. Hours here are too long.' Then she breathed in and added, 'So, until I get a dog, I swim.'

'You swim?' And he tried his absolute best not to think about what she looked like in a swimsuit.

'There's a swimming pool near where I live, so I try and do half a mile every morning. It only takes thirty minutes.' She lifted her arm to her nose and sniffed. 'So, if you ever think I smell of chlorine, that's why. But I do shower,' she joked.

'I'm sure you do.' He didn't let himself think on that subject any further. 'How many lengths is half a mile?'

'It depends entirely on the length of the pool. But for the one I go to, it's thirty-two lengths. There are quite a few people in at that time in the morning. There's no chat. Just in, swim and back out. There're a few kids too, mainly teenagers who are swimming competitively, so there's no one deliberately annoying me by swimming the wrong way.'

Now he couldn't help but laugh. 'You mean the people that swim widths, instead of lengths?'

She gave him a stern look. 'You know the way you hate jelly babies?' He nodded. 'That's the way I hate people swimming the wrong way.'

He laughed. 'Watch out, I might pay someone to come in and do that, just to annoy you.'

Her eyebrows went straight up. 'And I will fill your room with strings of jelly babies and tack them up on your wall like Christmas decorations.'

'This could be war,' he teased.

'It could.' She glanced at the clock on the wall. 'But it's too late. I need to get home. I have an imaginary cat to feed.'

Honestly? He didn't quite know what to make of Skye Campbell. But was he intrigued? You bet.

He watched as she picked up her bag and lifted her coat from the hook behind the door.

'Are you going to steal my sweeties if I leave you unsupervised in here?' she joked.

He stood up quickly, almost sad that she

wanted to leave. But as he glanced towards the office window, he could see it was black outside. Just how late was it?

She was just like him. A fellow workaholic. Whilst they might be at opposite sides of the spectrum for other things, at least at some points they overlapped.

'See you Monday,' he said as he headed out, back to his own office.

He could rush along to grab his stuff and walk out with her. But that seemed too forced. He'd found out so much more about his colleague to-night—there had even been some mild flirta-tion—and he wasn't entirely sure how he felt about that. Best just to leave things.

'Goodnight, Skye,' he said.

'Night, Jay,' she replied.

And for some weird reason that he couldn't explain, he watched her walk down the corridor until she reached the double doors to the lifts.

He was sorry to see her leave.

And for a man who'd vowed never to have a relationship at work again, that might be a trou-blesome thing.

CHAPTER THREE

'WHAT ON EARTH are you doing?'

It was just after seven in the morning and Skye had an array of bags at her feet. She stood behind the nurses' station in the ward, staring at the back wall. Her curls were pulled back in a ponytail, and he noticed the ends were slightly damp. She must have been up extra early for swimming.

She flung up her hands. 'I'm sorting out the advent calendar.'

Jay decided to stop peering over the station and walked around until he was beside her. 'Doesn't an advent calendar just have a bit of chocolate behind it every day?' He was bewildered at the paraphernalia at her feet.

'Amateur,' she scoffed. 'And those chocolate ones aren't real. I prefer the cardboard ones, you know, where they have a picture behind every window, like a robin, or a present, or a Christmas tree.'

'Anyway, it's not December yet.'

Skye dropped to her knees, picked up one of the bags and dumped the contents out on the floor. There was a whole array of small bags with numbers on them in a variety of Christmas colours.

'That's why I have to get things prepared. We're only two days away.'

He bent down and picked up a red bag with the number thirteen hand-stitched in green. 'What are these for?'

She waved her hand at the untouched wall. 'I hang them all up here in order, put things in them, and every day a staff member gets to open the bag for the day and the contents are their present.'

Jay stared at the small bag, opening it, and looked at her again. 'What on earth can you fit in here?'

This is where her face lit up. 'Oh, lots of things, they're all in here.' She gestured to another bag and he peered inside. Tiny perfume and aftershave, candles, a few decorations, some sweets from an exclusive chocolatier in Edinburgh, a bag with crystals, a knitted hat, some gloves and a tiny book.

He shook his head. 'Where did you get all this?'

'I buy them all year around. I know what people on the ward like. I've got something for everyone.'

'You've done all this yourself?'

Her smile just widened. 'Christmas is my thing. It's my absolute favourite time of year. I do one for the staff, and one for the patients.'

'Doesn't this cost you a fortune?' He was slightly stunned.

She waved a hand. 'As I said, I buy things all year round, so don't really notice. Here, help me pin up the bags in order, then I'll fill them.'

If anyone had told Jay Bannerman that he'd be pinning up bags on a wall at seven in the morning, he'd have thought they'd had some kind of weird dream. But instead, he bent down to sort out the bags in order and started pinning them to the wall.

'Won't we get in trouble for this?' he asked.

She gave a half-hearted shrug. 'Indira the ward sister doesn't mind. The maintenance guy sometimes has something to say about it, but I always have a secret gift stashed for him somewhere. So, he forgives me.'

'And you do this every year?' he asked incredulously.

She nodded. 'Of course. It's Christmas.' She shot him a wicked smile. 'I also have a number of Christmas dresses, earrings, a speaker to play Christmas music and a real love of the Christmas movie channels.'

He kept pinning bags to the wall and she started to fill them. 'When you've finished these ones,' she said, 'the patient ones are in the other bag.'

Her arm brushed against his and he automatically caught his breath.

'Are you always this bossy?' he teased.

She gave him a shocked look. 'I'm not bossy. I'm just a good organiser.' She took a breath. 'Anyhow, the guys here would wonder what was wrong if I didn't put up the calendar.'

He narrowed his gaze. 'Do you think you might be getting taken advantage of?'

'Grumpy Grinch,' she muttered under her breath, still smiling.

'I'm being serious,' he said, turning towards her, realising how close they actually were.

Since that late-night chat in her office, he'd sensed they were holding each other at arm's length slightly. Even now, when the ward was quiet, with some patients still sleeping, and the rest of the staff quietly going about their business, it seemed as if they were the only two around.

He caught a waft of her perfume. It was different from before. Lighter, but with a definite hint of Christmas. Was it trees?

He let out a laugh. 'Why do you smell of Christmas trees?'

She touched her hair, her eyes bright. 'Do I? Great, it's working. I thought it was just some kind of gimmick. I changed my shampoo. It's supposed to be Christmas Evergreen Woods.'

He put his hand over his mouth as he sneezed. 'Sorry.' But he couldn't help but laugh again. 'It's certainly working.'

He ducked into the nearby treatment room to wash his hands, before coming back out to pin up the patients' bags.

He picked up a few vouchers that Skye had left on the station. 'What are these for?'

'One is for Lleyton, the physio—that's his favourite coffee place—and other will be for Ronnie. He's an avid reader. It's for his favourite bookshop.'

'Ronnie? The man mountain?'

She wagged her finger. 'You mean Ronnie, the gentle giant.'

'I didn't take him for a reader.'

'I dare you to find a subject or author he hasn't read. The guy should be on mastermind with books as his specialist subject.'

She really had thought about everything. 'How do people know what number to pick?'

'Oh, I check the off duty and make sure everyone is scheduled to get their present on a day they're working. I leave little tags on the bags.'

Jay folded his arms. 'You really think about this.' It was a statement, rather than a question.

She folded her arms too, mimicking his stance. 'I was actually joking about you being a Grinch and a grump. But any second now I'll think that you'll refuse to dress up as Santa for the ward Christmas party.'

He froze, taking a few seconds to work out whether she was joking or not. But she couldn't hold it together and laughed out loud.

'Your face, it's a picture.' She playfully hit his arm. 'There's no way you'd get that job. It's Ronnie's. Every year.' She winked. 'I think he might even fight you for it.'

As they'd been talking, the ward was starting to get busier. More patients had woken up. Drug rounds had started. And one of the nursing staff appeared next to them with an observation chart in her hand. Almost everything was done electronically now, but clipboards with observation charts were still at the bottom of every bed.

The nurse, Ruby, handed it over. 'Leah's starting to run a temp and has tachycardia. Can someone listen to her chest again, and I'll get a urine sample and check that?'

Skye let out a low groan and looked over Jay's shoulder as he read the chart. 'Did she get a central line inserted yet for her chemo?'

Ruby nodded. 'I've checked that. Nothing obvious.'

Skye pulled her lilac stethoscope from around her neck. 'I'll listen to her chest. I'm pretty sure her chest infection has completely cleared, but I'll listen again.'

Jay nodded to Ruby. 'You'll let me know if anything shows in her urine. And can you observe her wound site every couple of hours, please? Last thing we want to do is stop the chemo, but if she's not fit we'll have to.'

Ruby nodded and disappeared.

There was another nurse on the computer at the station, so Jay headed into the nearest office to use another. It just so happened to be Skye's.

The phlebotomist was due in the ward soon, and he wanted to add another few things onto Leah's blood tests. The most dangerous thing for any patient was to develop sepsis. At this point he would put her on the potential pathway, which meant she would have regular obs, and be watched very carefully.

As he sat down at Skye's computer he noticed

two paper Christmas calendars on her desk, alongside two chocolate ones.

She walked in as he was inputting Leah's requirements. 'Chest is clear,' she said, and as Ruby walked in at her back she turned. 'Anything?'

Ruby shook her head. 'Nothing obvious when I dip-sticked her urine, but I'll send a sample down to the lab.'

He looked at them both. 'Potential sepsis pathway?' they said in unison.

It was oddly comforting. The staff in this ward knew exactly how dangerous things were for these highly vulnerable patients. He nodded. 'I've just ordered a few extra tests.'

Ruby nodded. 'I'm looking after Leah today, but I'll let Indira know too.'

The staff here worked twelve-hours shifts, and all staff needed breaks, so it was essential that someone co-ordinated the next few hours for Leah's care.

'Thanks,' he murmured as she left. He sat back, sighing. 'This is the last thing she needs.'

Skye agreed. 'We're both here all day. We can keep a close eye on her. I can cancel our meeting if you want?'

Jay looked at her. Today was his first online meeting with their counterparts in London,

South Africa and Chicago, where a parallel study was running.

'I hope we can avoid that,' he said. 'Instead of going to the IT suite, would you be happy if we just sat together in one of our offices here? That way, if there's any change in Leah's condition, we're right at hand.'

'Fine with me,' she said easily. 'I don't want anything happening to our girl.'

Our girl.

It was the way she said those words so easily. Jay wasn't always good with people—probably because he didn't like wasting time, and he didn't always do the niceties that could be expected.

But something about this place was affecting his manner. He found himself stopping to think before issuing sharp instructions. And all the staff here had gone out of their way to be friendly.

Before, at the Great Southern, whenever anyone had asked any kind of personal question it had always felt like prying. But back there he'd been dating a fellow doctor. He'd hated being part of the hospital gossip mill, and that's how it had always felt.

But just yesterday, someone had asked him a general question about running, then had given

Jay some routes through the city to try that he hadn't known about. Someone else had told him which petrol stations to avoid because they always overcharged, and another member of staff had casually told him in the canteen queue where to get the best coffee in the city.

Scottish people had a vibe very similar to the Irish. His accent gelled well here. People were interested to know what part of Ireland he was from, and everyone seemed to know a person who lived in a city or village near his own.

It was almost as if he was finally working in a place he could…breathe. Relax a little. Without looking over his shoulder to see who might be talking about him.

Maybe he was just a bit paranoid, but he'd walked in on a number of conversations about himself back at the Great Southern. First, when he was dating Jessica—then, when they'd split up—and then, when the whole hospital had suspicions about who she was dating now. He'd lost all of that when he'd come here, and it wasn't until now he realised what a relief that was.

Now, he was beginning to feel like part of a team. And those two simple words, *Our girl*, let a gentle heat spread through him.

Skye sat down opposite him. 'Pick your calendars.'

'What?'

She turned them around. 'I bought you one of each for your office. But—' she pointed to the chocolate one '—only to be used in an emergency.' Then she winked. 'And open my drawer.'

He looked at her suspiciously before pulling open her drawer to see a packet of chocolate digestives.

'Have to look after my colleague.' She beamed.

Something in him prickled. It would be easy. Easy to let himself flirt with this woman, and easy to be attracted to her. But that would take him back to the situation he was relieved to be away from.

'I don't really do Christmas calendars,' he said.

Skye paused, thinking for a few moments, then stood up. 'Oh no, you don't get to do that around here.'

'I don't get to not like Christmas calendars?'

She put her hands on her hips. 'You don't get to refuse a gift.'

Oh, no. And now he felt crummy.

He wasn't quite sure what to make of all this.

His brain was clear that he didn't ever want to have a relationship with a colleague again. He wanted his private life to be exactly that— private.

But from the moment he'd set foot on this ward he couldn't ignore what was straight in front of him. An attractive, intelligent, committed woman with fire in her belly. He could keep telling himself that he didn't like her, and wasn't attracted to her—but that wouldn't be true.

They'd fallen into flirtation the other night, and it had come too easily to them both.

Maybe this was all in his head. Maybe there had been no flirtation. But the cheeky smiles, winks and way that they gelled together was playing havoc with his senses.

And even when he tried to draw a little line in the sand, like now, she wasn't having it.

'You pick the one you like best. Advent calendars are clearly your thing. I will be happy to take what's left.'

'What's left?'

He nodded, knowing he hadn't made the situation any better. It might be better not to say anything at all. But he couldn't stay silent for long.

'We have to prepare for our meeting with your research colleagues,' he said. 'Somehow, I think our time would be better served preparing for that and keeping an eye on Leah, rather than worrying about Christmas decorations.'

It came out more cutting that he intended, but he was exasperated. He was here to do a job.

He needed to focus on that. The meeting today was important, and he would have thought Skye would be taking things more seriously. Even though her research project had gone through all the relevant ethics committee, at any point a research supervisor, such as himself, could ask for things to be called to a halt. Truth be told, he was yet to be convinced by the use of AI in tracking cancer growth reliably.

Skye's eyes widened for the merest second, then narrowed again. He'd annoyed her. And maybe things were better that way.

'That's the thing about women and their ability to multitask,' she said, her tone full of disdain. 'We can do all things well, at the *same* time.'

She picked up two of the advent calendars from his desk and left.

That was the moment he realised the chocolate calendar she'd left behind had a picture of the Grinch on it.

Skye was fuming. She'd thought that she and Jay were getting somewhere. She'd finally stopped inwardly swooning over his accent every time he spoke. His serious manner was starting to filter away, and then, in the blink of an eye, it was back.

She was beginning to think he was a Christmas hater.

Part of her brain was shouting at her, telling her to keep her research supervisor on side. But she didn't feel the need. The heart to heart they'd had the other night had surely shown him how passionate she was about this project. She knew she hadn't overlooked anything in her countless challenges through the ethics committees. There were no issues with her project—whether Jay Bannerman liked the concept or not.

She hung her own advent calendars on the wall. In two days, she could start opening the doors. It made her smile, no matter how annoyed she was. There was something magical about the countdown to Christmas.

She gave a little sigh and looked out her office window. Even though it was daytime, she knew that by nightfall the famous Christmas market would have started, the Christmas tree on the Mound would be lit up and the streets would be decorated.

She loved this time of year. But she'd been so busy that she hadn't had a chance to really enjoy the city's festive spirit yet. Walking the streets at night, with the lights around her, hearing her feet crunching on the ice forming beneath her, with a woolly hat pulled around her ears—it was one of her favourite things on earth.

In the next few days, she was definitely going to visit the market at night again. It just had to be done.

Her phone signalled, letting her know her meeting would be starting soon. She bit her lip. She had enough time to check on Leah first, but as she walked along the corridor, she could see that Jay had already beat her to the room. He was wearing a mask, apron and gloves, and was peeling back the dressing at her central line. It wasn't unusual for staff to wear protective equipment around patients who were immunosuppressed, so Skye grabbed an apron and mask for herself and hurried in.

Jay was talking in a low voice to Leah, who was lying back against her pillows. Her pallor was still obvious. The nurse was around the other side of the bed, checking Leah's temperature and blood pressure.

As Skye stepped up behind him, Leah had her eyes closed. She was listening to the melodic tones of his voice as he told her exactly what he was doing, and reassuring her along the way. He did have patient skills when he concentrated on it.

But Skye's attention was on the wound site.

As he pulled back the dressing, she could see the tiniest hint of red around the edges. She had to press her face closer, making Jay jerk a little as he clearly hadn't realised she was behind him.

'So, this is our site of infection?' she queried.

She heard him take a deep breath behind the mask. 'It could be, or it could just be a little irritation from the compounds in the central line. It's really too early to say, but I'm starting her on some broad-spectrum IV antibiotics.'

'That'll be her second set,' she murmured, knowing exactly what the ongoing problems were for patients who were immunosuppressed.

He nodded. 'We have to treat her symptoms. We both know I can't wait for all the lab results to come back. She has clear signs of infection somewhere.'

He nodded to the nurse to cover the wound site again, before removing his gloves and giving Leah's hand a squeeze. 'Leah, we're going to start some antibiotics again. We'll give them through your vein so there is chance of them working quicker, and hopefully you'll start feeling a bit better soon.'

'I'll give your mum and dad a quick call. Explain what's happened and that we'll talk to them later today.' Her eyes went to the clock as

Jay electronically prescribed the medicine on a nearby tablet.

Since they hadn't agreed what office to work in, Skye wasn't surprised when, as soon as she replaced the phone on her desk, Jay walked in with his laptop in his hands. 'We've already connected,' he said, pulling a seat up next to her, as he sat the laptop down.

She could see the faces of her colleagues in London, South Africa and Chicago. A few looked slightly tired, but it was hard to coordinate appropriate time zones across the world.

Skye was caught a bit off guard, but settled in her chair and took a breath. 'Shall we do introductions?'

The camera on the laptop required her and Jay to sit close together, their shoulders almost brushing. She fixed a smile on her face. 'So, you've already met Dr Bannerman, who will be my research supervisor for this project, and is also our new temporary Director of Oncology at the Great Northern Hospital. He previously had the same role at our Southern counterpart.'

All colleagues took a few moments to introduce themselves, and she could see Jay start to pick up. He recognised research studies that they had been involved in, and they in turn recognised some of his published studies.

The conversation quickly turned to the actual samples collected. There were over eight hundred, all from a variety of different forms of cancer. A pathologist joined at this point to explain that each sample was examined by three different pathologists, to ensure agreement on the cancer type, stage and any anomalies. Cancer journeys were then plotted in real life, and once new sample cancer cells had been confirmed by type and stage, AI plotted their likely path. This was the part where Jay became most vocal. He questioned the best pathways of care for each journey, and if patients were being given their optimum path. He talked about the new data learned every day from cancer, and if changing treatment types would affect the results of their study.

Skye understood that. He didn't want any patients to be compromised because they were part of the study. She didn't either. And although most cancers had guidelines for stages and treatments, every person had to be treated as an individual. Their counterparts in Chicago and South Africa talked about their own guidelines and when they would make a different decision based on a patient's presentation. A few specific patients were brought to the table for discussion. There were no concerns about the pathway decisions, but there were questions about whether it was feasible for them to remain part of the study. These things always happened in research studies, and were necessary to ensure the studies remained reliable and robust.

Skye herself became more animated as the discussion continued. The AI mapping so far was exceeding expectations for breast and renal cancer, and they spent a long time debating why these types of cancer appeared easier to predict. By the time the meeting came to an end, she honestly felt exhausted.

She didn't even try to hide it as she slumped back in her chair, lifting the paperwork from one of the cases that AI had plotted and predicted. She looked at Jay. 'Do we really think that breast and renal cancer are easier to predict, or are they just easier to predict for AI because it has so much data behind it?'

Jay looked at her in interest. 'What do you mean?' His words sounded a little sharp, and she wondered what he had actually thought of the meeting.

She ran her fingers across the page. 'Look at how many vectors it has taken into consideration. My brain couldn't even begin to compute that many things.'

He made a noise. She wasn't quite sure if it was in agreement or dispute.

She should be happy. Jay had taken part in his first meeting of the research project. And although he'd asked questions, most of which she felt were valid, she was hoping he would be more reassured by now, and certainly a bit more enthusiastic.

She gestured to some patient files. 'Think of the difference we can make to these patients whose cells have been categorised now.'

'I'm not ready to think like that yet,' he said. 'I still want to look at margins of error.'

'It's all covered in the research proposal and the plans. The data is there.' She was becoming a bit hostile, and she didn't really like that, but the bottom line was that Jay Bannerman was annoying her.

Then he ran his fingers through that slightly too-long hair and glanced over at her with those brown eyes. Did he know how good looking he was? Was he trying to irritate her?

'Take your time,' she said smoothly as she stood up. 'I'll go and check on Leah.'

His mouth opened, but she watched as he visibly stopped himself from answering. It was likely he wanted to check on Leah himself. But she was a doctor on this ward, and she didn't need his permission to check on her own patient.

She strode along the corridor, irritated. Her mind was spinning in circles. Was he going to throw a spanner in the works for her research? Did he even really understand it? Why couldn't he be as enthusiastic about it as she was? Her stomach clenched as she turned into Leah's room, meeting the nurse at the door.

'No change,' the nurse said. 'I've been monitoring her wound site. It's not showing obvious signs of infection. The first lot of IV antibiotics went in with no issues, and she's due the second set in an hour.'

Skye kept her voice low. 'Any sign of improvement?'

The nurse shook her head. 'Not yet. But there's not really been enough time.' She looked at Skye. 'Could you phone the lab and see if there's any news on the potential urine infection?'

Skye nodded, glad to have something to do, but knowing that her colleague was trying to placate her.

It was worth it. The call to the lab meant a diagnosis of a more unusual urinary tract infection, which needed specific antibiotics. Skye listened carefully, then telephoned a colleague who was a urologist to ask for some advice on the treatment. Some antibiotics could affect patients with a weakened immune system more severely, and she wanted to tread carefully with Leah. The last thing she wanted was to make her sicker than she already was.

She prescribed the new antibiotics, along with some anti-sickness meds, and phoned the pharmacy to make sure the ward would have them on site in the next hour.

When she went back to check on Leah, she found Jay in the room talking to her. Leah was slightly more awake than before, although she still looked exhausted.

She gave Skye a weak smile. 'Dr Jay was just telling me about what he used to get up to back in Ireland with his sister.'

Skye's eyes widened. 'Well, that's a story I haven't heard. Should I pull up a chair?'

Colour heated his cheeks—she couldn't really imagine him telling personal stories to a patient.

But for the first time in a few days, Leah was smiling. 'I told him that I loved horses, and he told me about him and his sister stealing one from the farm next door.'

He sat up straighter in his chair, and she could almost see all his defences clicking into place.

Skye's smile was completely genuine. 'Oh,

do tell.' She sat down and crossed one leg over the other.

For a second, his eyes went to her legs.

No, she hadn't imagined that.

'We…were adventurous kids,' he said easily. 'My sister was annoyed she hadn't got a toy horse for Christmas. So, we decided to steal a real one.'

'That's a bit of jump,' said Skye.

Jay shook his head. His accent even thicker. 'Na, the actual bit of a jump was the hedge between our farms. Our mams and dads didn't like each other. We had to climb the hedge to get over to their place. And our Marian, she didn't just want the pony—because they had a number of horses over there. No, she wanted the palomino—the golden and white beauty that was their pride and joy.'

'And did you actually steal it?' Skye leaned forward. She was fascinated with this insight into Jay's childhood.

He pulled a face and waggled his hand. 'Eh… we borrowed it. Just for half an hour or so.' He shrugged. 'Then we got caught.'

Leah put her hand up to her mouth. 'What happened when you got caught?'

'No, wait.' Skye held up her hand. 'How did you actually steal it?'

She nodded as the nurse walked in with the new IV infusion bag.

'They had a big old house. We had to duck under their windows to get to the stables. The stables were kind of at an angle. So, no windows from the house directly looked on to them. It was easy enough to get into the stables, we just had to take Whitmore Shores out of his stall. The bridle was right there. And we could both put a bridle on in our sleep.'

'The horse was called Whitmore Shores?' asked Leah, her brow furrowed.

He exchanged a glance with Skye as she realised what that meant. 'You stole a race horse?' she asked.

He gave a small grimace. 'We called him Goldie.' He sighed. 'So, we put the bridle on, and Marian got on his back and just took off across the fields.'

'Did she have a saddle?' asked Leah, her eyes wide. It was the most awake and focused she'd been all day.

He shook his head. 'She didn't need one. Marian was always a natural on horseback.'

'Didn't she fall off?'

'I can honestly say I've never seen my sister fall off a horse.'

'Wait a minute,' said Skye, 'how did you get caught?'

He waved a hand. 'Oh, that's easy. Marian decided the fields weren't enough and she wanted to take the horse over to our house. So, instead of picking a way across the fields again, she marched the horse right past their front window and down their driveway. It took Mr Rogers about ten seconds to be out of his front door, roaring his lungs out at us.'

Skye and Leah started to laugh at once. Jay laughed too, wagging his finger at them both. 'And the lesson learned that day was, don't take Marian Bannerman with you if you want to pull off a heist.'

He looked a bit wistful for a moment. 'I miss that house.'

'They don't live there anymore?'

He shook his head. 'They live in Brighton now, and they absolutely love it. I keep expecting them to tell me they're moving back home, but my sister is over here too now.' He tapped his eye. 'I think they stay in this country because they think they can keep an eye on us.'

Leah was laughing now, clearly distracted and liking the chat.

Skye's eyes went back to the IV. The nurse had connected it whilst they were talking and the medicine was running in. She'd left a medicine cup next to Skye.

She picked it up and held it out to Leah. 'Take this for me. It's a medicine to stop you being sick.'

Leah frowned. 'I've not been sick.'

Jay replied before Skye could. 'Your new medicine is quite powerful and can make some people sick, we're just trying to stop you feeling like that.'

Leah looked at the fluid-filled bag. 'So, do you know what it is yet?'

Jay nodded. 'You've got a urine infection, and it's one that responds best to the medicine that's in the drip.' It was clear he'd read the lab report, and the notes that Skye had put in Leah's file. He really didn't miss much. And Skye wasn't sure if that made her happy or sad.

She'd always thought of herself as meticulous and thorough. Why on earth would she not admire those traits in someone else?

Jay leaned forward and started telling Leah another story. He was watching her, monitoring her whilst this new drug infused. And it seemed that, whilst he did that, he didn't seem to mind sharing a little part of himself.

It was a new side to Dr Bannerman. He'd mentioned he wasn't too good with patients. And their first encounter had seemed a little clunky. But maybe he wasn't as bad as he thought.

Or maybe he'd been affected by new surroundings, or a new job.

Whatever it was, the man she was watching now—relaxed in his chair, small laughter lines around his eyes and completely engaged with their patient—was extraordinary to watch.

She was quite sure that Leah wouldn't know the real reason they were both there. And that was just as important.

Skye settled back, smiling. She was quite happy to watch the Jay Bannerman show, and learn as much as she could.

CHAPTER FOUR

IT WAS FINALLY the first of December and, as Jay approached the ward, he didn't know what to expect.

He was slightly later this morning, having had to attend a consultant meeting with the medical director, and as he walked onto the ward it was slightly quieter than he'd expected. Yes, he could hear Christmas music playing, but it was low and subdued. He could see that the first little advent bag had been taken down, and couldn't remember which staff member's name had been attached. He was gradually getting to know people a little better, becoming familiar with all their names and quirks.

Connie was behind the desk as he walked up.

'What's wrong?' he asked, scanning the ward for more people. He could see that some patients were up at the side of their beds, and nursing and physio staff were in the six-bedded rooms.

Connie gave him a sad smile. 'Mr Kerr was

admitted this morning. He's a long-time patient. On his third type of cancer. He lost his wife last year and is now on his own. He's not looking good at all.'

She tapped a tablet, bringing up the man's records, and handed it to Jay. 'We all love him. He's such a nice man.' She gave a long sigh and looked out one of the windows. 'We hate it when it gets to this stage with someone we've looked after for years. It's just so hard.'

Jay scanned the notes. Frank Kerr was in his late seventies. He'd had bowel, lung and now bladder cancer. Each one treated in succession, and to all intents and purposes cured. But that was the thing about cancer. Cells could be like spiderwebs instead of round capsules, and could reach unpredictable places.

Unpredictable. He wondered if Frank Kerr was part of the study. He'd have to ask Skye later.

'Where is Skye?' he asked.

Connie pressed her lips together for a moment.

'What is it?' he asked.

'She's with Mr Kerr. He was one of her father's friends. He was a good bit older, but I think they'd worked together.'

'Oh.' It was all he could say. He could only imagine how this was hitting her. Should he ask to take over Mr Kerr's care? He didn't want to offend her, but this might all be a bit too close to home. 'I'll go and join her.'

He turned to go and Connie pushed something towards him. It was a plate with some slightly lop-sided scones. 'Take these for Frank. Cheese scones are his favourites.'

Jay gave a nod and lifted the plate, watching the scones precariously skid around as if they were on a skating rink. He concentrated, tucking the tablet under one arm, eyes focused on the plate as he made his way to the patient's room.

The first thing that struck him was how thin Mr Kerr was. Was this normal for him? The second thing he noticed was that Mr Kerr and Skye's hands were intertwined.

He moved forward and put the scones on Mr Kerr's bed table.

'Hi there,' he said in a soft voice. 'I'm Jay Bannerman, one of the new doctors. Connie sent me to give you some scones.'

Frank had the palest blue eyes, which opened as he smiled. 'She's an angel.'

Skye looked up. Her hand hadn't moved. She clearly wasn't embarrassed about how close she was to this patient. Jay nodded to the scones. 'Can I get one of our support workers to bring you some tea to go with the scones? Then maybe we can have a chat about your care.'

He could see Skye visibly bristle. 'I'm looking after Frank,' she said.

He put a hand on her shoulder. It was a friendly gesture, but also one to remind her where she was. 'Of course you are, Dr Campbell, but we're a team here, and I gather Frank's a special guest. I want to make sure I'm up to date on all his needs, so we can make him comfortable.'

He wasn't trying to tell her off, and was careful with his words, but her shoulders slumped a little. She squeezed Frank's hand. 'I'll get us tea, then I'll be back.'

She gave a tiny nod of her head to Jay and he followed her to the ward kitchen. As the boss, there was a whole host of things he should say. All about trying to keep a line between themselves and the patient, and about looking after friends who end up in the ward. But he went with the most important.

'Skye, are you all right?'

She shook her head as she opened the cupboard to pull out cups. 'No,' she said, her voice shaky.

'What can I do to help?' He put his hand on her arm. It wasn't just her voice that was shaky, her hand was trembling too. 'Let me make the tea.'

He gently moved her sideways, finding the rest of the equipment and getting water from the HydroBoil.

She dipped her head as he worked, her voice broken. 'I can't believe how he's deteriorated. There was a package of care in place for him. He looks like he hasn't eaten in weeks. No wonder the cancer has taken hold. He's got nothing left to fight with.'

She started to sob and shake. Jay put his arms around her, pulling her close.

He didn't say anything. He just held her in place, rubbing her back gently as she sobbed.

He'd never seen her upset like this. One of the support workers came to walk in, saw Jay's gentle shake of the head and discreetly walked away.

Little flags shot up in his brain. Would people talk? Would rumours start? But he took a breath. Petty rumours be damned. Whilst it might not be for everyone, if a colleague needed a hug, he would do it.

Her sobbing quietened, and she pulled back a bit, her face streaked with mascara, part of her make-up on the shoulder of his white coat.

'Sorry,' she breathed.

'Don't be,' he replied, then took another breath. 'What do you want me to do? As your boss I should ask you if you want me to take over Frank's care? I don't want you to feel compromised in any way.'

She bit her lip. She still hadn't moved fully away from him—his arm was still at her waist. 'My first reaction is to be angry and say no.' She waited a moment then shook her head. 'But I do feel too attached. I want him to be comfortable and have a good end. I want to make sure his wishes are in place. But…' She paused a moment, then nodded. 'But I know Frank is terminal. I know this will be his last visit. I don't want anyone to have a chance to insinuate anything about this unit.'

The thoughts were clearly forming in her head as she spoke. 'I'd prefer it if you could prescribe his meds, and review his pain relief. I'm not a family member, but last time around Frank's son was in Japan. I'm happy to talk to him, to let him know it's time to come over.'

She sighed, and held up her hands. 'You know the first time he came in I didn't really remember him. He recognised me straight away and asked me if I was Evan Campbell's daughter. He could tell me about parties he'd come to at the family home, and once he did that, I remembered playing in my back garden with his son. And he told me a million stories of my dad from when they were young—things my dad never got a chance to tell me. He and his wife were so close. They did everything together.' She put her hand on her chest. 'I just think he doesn't want to be here without her.'

Jay nodded. 'I noticed in his notes that he told his GP he'd had symptoms for months before he attended. He knew what he had, Skye. Let me talk to him. Let me be the independent person that you can't possibly be. Let me talk to him about treatment—which I think he'll refuse—and his end-of-life care.'

'I want to help,' she said quickly.

'And you will,' he reassured her. 'But let's have a clean line about who his doctor is, and who makes medical decisions.'

She pressed her lips together. 'I hate this.'

'Then let me help you.'

They'd had this whole conversation face to face, only inches apart. It was intensely personal. But so was the subject matter.

'Thank you,' she said breathily, their eyes connecting.

They stood there for probably a moment more than they should. He didn't want to lift his hand away from her waist, or the other from her elbow. He hated that her face was tear-streaked. He hated that she felt in this position. But it was natural. He'd had patients that he'd treated for more than ten years himself, and they almost became friends.

He was the boss. He had to let her be a friend without compromising her role as doctor. And he could do that.

She wiped her face. 'I better clean up before we go back in.'

'I'll make this tea,' he said with a smile.

'Frank likes builder's tea,' she said, her eyes bright with tears, 'so to be sure to let it stew. Oh, and butter for the scones.'

She disappeared to the toilets and Jay organised the tea, putting everything on a tray.

'I could have done that.' One of the healthcare support workers was bringing back some dishes to the kitchen.

'It's fine,' he said over his shoulder, as he headed back into the ward area and Frank's room.

Skye joined them a few moments later, and once Frank had started to eat his scone and drink his tea, they had a long chat about his life and wishes.

Every doctor wanted to wave a magic wand and cure every patient. And whilst treatments mainly got better year on year, and research studies helped find out more and more about the disease, sometimes there reached an end point for patients.

Jay was always respectful of patients' wishes. But his heart strings tugged when Frank said he'd wished he'd just slipped away at home with no fuss. He was emaciated, and frail. He didn't always take his medicines, as his water tablets had him up too many times at night. His package of care had dwindled—the council didn't have enough staff to maintain everyone at home.

Skye kept her cool, although he saw her wiping away a few angry tears.

'You should have told me, Frank,' she said. 'I could have come and helped you.'

Frank gave her a sad smile. 'But I didn't want you to, Skye. I wanted you to stay here, and do the job you do, helping those that want help.'

She reached out and took his hand again. She might not be family, but she was the closest that Frank Kerr had to family until his son got here.

In his head, Jay got a vision of a younger version of Skye—how she'd coped with her own father's death. It gripped him like a vice. He was sure this would bring back memories, and trauma, and he wanted to make sure he looked out for her.

He might only have been here a few weeks, but he already could sense the dynamic around the whole unit, and Skye was a huge part of that. Her normally sunny demeanour seemed to rub off on everyone. He'd yet to hear anyone say a bad word about her—even in jest—and from what he'd witnessed her colleagues seemed to admire her.

Today was the first time he'd seen her without her normal festive spirit. She hadn't even mentioned Christmas.

He made a mental note to try and brighten her mood later. These would be a hard few days. And, whilst he could take care of Mr Kerr, he wasn't quite sure how much he could take care of Skye Campbell.

'You finished?'

Jay appeared in her doorway with his jacket already on and zipped up. It wasn't too late, only eight o'clock, but she couldn't believe how tired she was.

'I'm just finishing a few things,' she said with a weak smile.

He walked over and looked down at her notes. 'Anything that can't wait until tomorrow?'

Now she was a bit confused. She looked up. 'Why?'

'Because it's been a tough day, and I wanted

to make it a bit better for you.' He gave a wink. 'I'm not always the Grinch, you know.'

She pushed her chair back and stretched out her tired legs. She was intrigued. 'What did you have in mind?'

'Do you have warm clothes?'

She let out a laugh and pulled out a drawer stuffed with hats, scarves and gloves in an array of colours, then pointed to her bright pink wool coat hanging behind the door.

'I think I might be able to manage that.' She grabbed some items from the drawer, slid on her coat and put her bag across her body. 'This better be good,' she teased.

'It will be. Have you said goodnight to Frank?'

She nodded. 'He's already sleeping.'

'Then let's go.'

He led her out the hospital and along the main road towards the centre of town. 'First time in Edinburgh at Christmas,' he said. 'So, I thought I would ask the expert to show me the Christmas lights.'

Her face lit up and her body seemed to straighten. She glanced at him, a renewed sparkle in those green eyes. 'Oh, I think I can manage that. Just how far do you think you can walk?'

'Is that a challenge?' he asked, his smile widening. It was clear this had been the right thing to do. Her mood had lifted instantly once they got outside the hospital.

'It could be,' she teased. 'We'll just need to see if you're up to it.'

'Well,' he said, 'in that case, let's start this night the right way. What's your festive drink? Hot chocolate or mulled wine?'

The streets around them had a number of other people out admiring the festive lights, and there were a few street carts along the way, with a few more regular wooden stands offering a range of food and drinks.

'Mulled wine is for nearer Christmas,' she mused, breathing out a long visible breath in the cold air. 'Hot chocolate would certainly be welcome.'

They joined a short queue for hot chocolate with marshmallows, flakes and cream, and she was soon sipping as they walked.

Skye had put on a grey woollen hat that had a dog emblem on the front. He nodded at her. 'So, is that the kind of dog you would like—a Scottie?'

She sighed. 'Dog talk. My favourite kind of dog.' She put her hand to her hat. 'I would like a Scottie. But I would also consider a Labrador, because of their good nature, a spaniel for their cute faces, or a cockapoo because I think I might have a similar nature.'

He laughed as he looked at her. 'I'm not entirely sure how to react that one, so I'll just let it go.'

She kept smiling as she sipped. 'You know my favourite actor, Patrick Stewart, fosters pit bulls in America, to show how loving and good-natured they actually are—I'd think about one of them too. Apparently, they are the dogs always left at the shelters.' She turned to him as they walked. 'Have you ever had a dog?'

'We looked after our next-door neighbour's dog when they emigrated to Australia. It was about six months before the dog could join them. It was a mongrel, some kind of collie mix, and Dora had wandered in and out of our house since they'd got her. I think she got fed there, then came to ours to get fed too.'

Skye nodded, her dark green eyes barely visible beneath the edge of her hat. 'Dogs are far more intelligent than we give them credit for.'

They continued down the streets, heading for St Andrew Square, where most of the buildings had their own light displays.

As they rounded the corner, Skye let out a sigh. 'One of my favourite places at Christmas. I could stay here all night and look at the lights.'

He smiled. The stress and anxiety that had been written all over her face had vanished. She was back to her normal smiley self, and whilst at first he'd thought her naturally bright demeanour would annoy him, it had only taken a few hours of its absence to make him realise what an essential part of her it was.

'Glad you're feeling a bit better,' he said lowly.

She slid her arm into his as if it were the most natural thing in the world. St Andrew Square was busier, and it kept them together, but Jay couldn't ignore the little buzz going up his arm. They stopped into a bar and had a beer, then headed up towards the castle.

There was a special light show on at Edinburgh Castle for the Christmas period and hospital staff had free tickets. They showed their passes and went on in.

It wasn't just lights, it was sounds and history. They followed the light trail to the castle courtyard. Depending on where you stood, you could watch a number of different stories take place. They watched a tale about the castle's history and battles fought, another about Scottish mythical beasts like the kelpies and Nessie, another was more like a party, sharing snapshots of artists who had performed at Edinburgh Castle, and the last story was around Scotland's most famous queen—Mary Queen of Scots.

They then followed a light tunnel, with white and red lights arched above them, and a dramatic spinning earth at the bottom, giving the illusion that they were actually in space, looking down from above.

'Wow,' Skye gave her head a little shake, 'I think I'm seeing stars after that one.'

She had left her hand where it was, slid through his arm, and Jay had seen several people looking at them. He knew they looked like a couple, and it was doing curious things to his brain. One part was thinking how nice it was, and how normal this all felt. The other part was shouting, warning him about his history of dating a colleague and how that all felt for him. Having his humiliation played out in front of everyone he worked with, and the whole hospital thinking they were entitled to know his and Jessica's business. That experience was hard to push aside.

He'd vowed not to walk that path again, and yet here he was, a few weeks after starting his new job, arm in arm with a new colleague in Edinburgh.

It went against everything he'd told himself. But being around Skye was…special.

He already knew parts of her history that he wasn't sure she shared with everyone. He'd watched her passion for her patients, and he'd seen her fall apart knowing she was going to watch someone she cared about die imminently.

'Hey,' someone said and they both jumped.

A small woman in a bright red coat was next to them, clutching the hand of a primary-school-age child.

'Hey, Roseann,' said Skye brightly.

Jay watched as Roseann's eyes went from one to the other, obviously taking in how close they looked.

Skye bent down to talk to the kid. 'Hi, Fletcher, are you enjoying the show?'

The boy nodded enthusiastically.

'Did you use the hospital tickets?' Skye asked as she stood back up.

'Aren't they great? It's about time there was some kind of bonus for working in the health service,' said Roseann, before leaning towards Skye. 'Heard the latest gossip?'

Skye gave an anxious glance at Jay before she shook her head. Jay knew exactly what was wrong. Skye didn't seem like the gossip type.

Roseann beamed and spoke in a not-so-low voice, even though she glanced around to see if anyone was listening. 'You know that Poppy Evans is pregnant?'

Skye gave a careful nod. 'Yes.' Jay had no idea who they were talking about.

'Word on the street is that the father of the baby is Dylan Harper, her fellow neurosurgeon.'

Skye's mouth dropped open, but she tried to cover it up. 'Well, I guess the only person who really knows that is Poppy. It's not really for us to say.'

'Of course not,' said Roseann conspiratorially. 'But wouldn't they make a nice couple?'

'I suppose,' said Skye with caution. Thankfully, Fletcher tugged his mother's hand and pulled her in another direction.

'Best be going,' said Roseann. 'See you at work.' She waved as she walked away.

Jay waited a few moments before he looked at Skye. 'What was all that about?'

'Hospital gossip,' she said uncomfortably. 'I hate it.'

It was like something washed over him. Relief. 'I have no idea who the people are she was talking about.'

'Good,' Skye replied, 'then you won't pass gossip on.' She stopped for a second and looked thoughtful. 'They would be a good-looking couple though.' Then she shook her head and smiled. 'None of my business.'

They started to walk again, finishing the light show in the castle and leaving by the main exit.

'Want another drink?' he asked, feeling hopeful.

There was a second of hesitation from her. 'Coffee. I'd like coffee. I'm getting cold again.'

They found a nearby street vendor and ordered two coffees, taking them over to a small bench under a tree.

'I've had a wonderful night,' she breathed, the steam from her coffee mixing with her breath in the air.

'I'm glad,' he said simply, trying not to stare at her too hard. She was beautiful in the warm lights from the nearby shop fronts. It pulled out the green in her eyes, and the darkness from the strands of hair that had escaped from her hat.

She lowered her head. 'Today was harder than normal. I care about all our patients. But seeing how much Frank had deteriorated shocked me. The same happened with my dad, but it seemed much more gradual.'

Jay nodded and, after a moment, slipped a hand around her back. 'I could see how it affected you. Here's hoping his son arrives soon.'

She leaned into him. 'I think he's honestly just waiting for his son to get here.'

'But until then, he has you. He obviously values the relationship you've had.'

Her head rested against his shoulder, and he got a small waft of her amber perfume. It suited her. Warm, rich-smelling, like a big hug.

This was the first time Jay had felt a connection to someone in so long. Even with Jessica, their last year together had almost seemed automatic. The romance and fun had fallen by the wayside. Work had overtaken everything.

But he hadn't had a chance for that to happen here. And all he could really think about was this beautiful woman at his side. The heat seeping through his coat from her to him. The fact he really just wanted to take her in his arms and…

Jay moved, just slightly, and her face tilted upward towards his.

Their lips met naturally, gently at first, and then as if they were feeling their way—with more passion.

Her hand came up to his cheek, and he slid his hand around her back, up and into her hair.

Their bodies shifted towards each other as their kiss deepened. He could taste the coffee on her lips. Feel the warmth of their bodies next to each other. For a second, he wished they were a million miles away from a public place. His lips moved from hers, first to her ear, and then to her neck. She was still holding on tightly, not letting go.

Then their lips naturally came together again, and heat started to spread across his chest and down his body. He would happily sit here all night kissing this woman.

Then Skye drew in a sharp breath and pulled back. Her pupils were dilated, her cheeks flushed.

'What?' he asked. 'What's wrong?' The pull-back had been sudden, as if there had been a shout, or she'd been hit by something.

She blinked and bit her lip, her eyes darting all over the place—anywhere but meeting his.

'This was a bad idea,' she said suddenly.

His stomach plummeted.

She stood up quickly, but placed a hand on his shoulder when he went to stand up too. 'No, don't.' Her voice was firm. 'I need to go home. Get some beauty sleep. I want to be up early in the morning and get back to see Frank.'

Jay went to stand again but her hand was firm.

'I'll walk you,' he offered, but she shook her head.

'No. I don't live too far, and I've walked these streets alone for years. I'll be fine.' Then she took a breath. 'Please, just let me go alone. I'll text you when I'm home.'

She started walking briskly away, dodging the other people on the streets until her pink coat and grey hat were lost in the crowd.

Jay felt frozen. What had he done? What had gone wrong? He stared down at their empty coffee cups before standing and putting them in a nearby rubbish bin.

It had been Skye who'd been the one to take his arm and to lean against him. She'd seemed so comfortable in his company all night. And she'd responded to his kiss in a way that made him know he hadn't been the only one thinking about it.

Jay stood and stretched his back. Stared in the direction she'd gone. He wanted to go after her, to talk to her again. But she'd asked him not to, so he would respect her wishes. Would he worry if she didn't text to say she was home safe? Of course he would. But he didn't know her address, and it would only be his place to raise an issue if she didn't appear at work tomorrow.

He sighed, shaking his head as he walked back towards his own place, his feet crunching on the pavements. All he could see right now were visions of her face throughout the night. When she'd smiled, the sparkle in her eyes. And when she'd been sad, the way his only thought had been to comfort her.

As he kept walking, the thoughts kept circling. It had been a long time since he'd thought about any woman this way, and that confused him. They'd only known each other a short time, and they'd kissed once. This wasn't like him. Not at all.

As he approached his front door, his phone sounded. He pulled it out. One word.

Home x

He gave a smile as he opened the door. Who knew if that kiss even meant something—or if it meant nothing at all.

What he did know for sure was what he'd dream about tonight. And that was a woman called Skye.

CHAPTER FIVE

EVEN THOUGH IT was early when he reached the ward next day, Skye had still beat him to it.

'She been here long?' he asked the ward sister.

Indira gave a sad nod. 'She's been here since about six. But Mr Kerr's son's plane is due to land about eleven this morning. So he should be here shortly after that.'

Jay gave a nod, not wanting to intrude on her time with Mr Kerr. He sat down next to Indira and took Mr Kerr's chart. 'Any concerns about his chest, pressure areas, urine output?'

Indira shook her head. 'All fine. His IV line tissued last night and had to be re-sited, but that was it.' She gave a smile. 'He did say that "everything hurt". But it's likely that his cancer might have moved to his bones.'

'Have we started an infusion yet for his pain?' Jay knew that bladder cancer could affect surrounding organs, even the bones in his pelvis.

'I was waiting for you to come in to talk about it.'

Jay nodded, drawing up the prescribing regime that they normally used for terminal patients. It gave them a low and steady amount of painkiller, with a chance for the patient to supplement themselves with the push of a button.

'Do you want me to go in and talk to him about this?'

Indira shook her head. 'I'll set it up and get it started. I think Skye will be fine to explain this to him.'

Jay paused for a moment. 'Once you've got that set up, let's go over the rest of the patients she normally would deal with—and I'm happy to speak to Mr Kerr's son if she's not comfortable doing it. They knew each other as kids, it might be difficult for her.'

Indira's head tilted to the side, and she gave him a cross between a curious glance and a warm smile. 'She seems to have opened up to you.'

He felt a small wave of panic. Had that person they'd met last night—Roseann—told people she'd seen them together? To be honest, he wouldn't be surprised in the slightest, but he hadn't been entirely sure she would have recognised him as a doctor from here.

The stare from Indira was making him feel as if he were under the spotlight, but maybe he was imagining it.

'She told me a little of how she knew Mr Kerr,' was all he replied in explanation.

'Okay,' was Indira's response as she left to go and set up the infusion pump.

Jay spent the next few hours examining the ward patients who needed reviews, checking over test results when required, and answering a few queries from GPs. He walked around to the day unit, to see those who came in for daily chemotherapy, and made sure everything was problem-free before he headed back to the ward.

As he arrived, he saw Skye hugging a tall, thin man as she left Mr Kerr's room. She walked down to the nurse's station, clearly blinking back tears.

'Mr Kerr's son?' he asked.

'Jason,' she said in croaky voice.

'Need me to talk to him, to do anything?'

She shook her head firmly. 'I've done it. He knows everything he needs to know, and now they just need some time together.'

Jay licked his lips, wondering if she wanted some space or not.

'I've seen all the ward patients, and those in day care. How do you feel about an early lunch?'

For a moment his heart was frozen, wondering if he might see a flash of panic in her eyes.

But instead, she just gave him a grateful nod. 'Yes, please.'

They headed down to the canteen, grabbed some hot drinks and bacon rolls, and found a table in the corner of the room.

Once they were seated, Jay didn't wait. 'I wanted to apologise,' he said quickly.

'Apologise?'

He nodded. 'For last night. I didn't mean to upset you, or step over a line. It was never my intention to offend you.'

Skye blinked and sat for a few seconds, trying to decide what to say. She wasn't quite sure where to go with this.

Sure, she had made excuses and left hastily last night, and it was likely odd, given they'd had such a nice evening together. But she'd just been shellshocked by what that kiss had actually done to her. What it had actually *awoken* in her. She hadn't actually expected him to apologise for the best kiss she'd had in her life.

'I think I should tell you something,' he continued.

Uh oh. Her stomach gave an uneven flip. That didn't sound good. She licked her lips. 'What?'

'I don't know how much you might have heard about me on the grapevine.' Jay looked extremely uncomfortable.

'Nothing,' she replied. There had been a few rumours, and she knew he'd been known as Dr Grumpy down south, but she had no idea why.

He took a deep breath, and she sensed he was a little relieved. Something flicked in her brain from last night. She'd spent her whole time thinking about the kiss since then, but something had just jarred her. When they'd met Roseann, and she'd clearly been gossiping. Jay had looked a little wary. It was clear he was just as uncomfortable with that sort of thing as she was.

'When I worked at the Southern,' he started, 'I was engaged to another doctor for five years.'

Skye shifted a little uncomfortably in her chair, not entirely sure she wanted to hear about another woman.

'We'd agreed to a long engagement—neither of us wanted to rush into marriage. But, last year, she broke it off suddenly. Then, a few weeks ago, she announced her new engagement to a guy we both worked with. I'd been uncomfortable already in the hospital.'

He paused and looked at her. 'When you have a relationship with anyone inside the hospital, the whole place thinks it's their business to have an opinion on it. I never liked it. I like my private life to be just that—private. And then, when it was clear that our relationship was over, and it became pretty obvious that she was likely dating him whilst still engaged to me, I just felt that everyone had their eyes on me, and that most people had likely been talking about me behind my back. Probably saying what a fool I was.'

'Oh, Jay, I'm sorry. That's horrible.'

He stared at his coffee cup for a moment. 'It is,' he agreed, then pressed his lips together. He leaned his head on one hand. 'Trouble is,' he said in that lilting accent, 'when you've likely been the talking point in your place of work, it makes your defences go up.' He raised his eyebrows. 'I might have got a bit of a reputation for being grumpy at work, and standoffish. But I just didn't want my business to become the hospital's grapevine. I stopped going to nights out, or anything like that, because I just hated the thought of being made a fool of again.'

Skye gulped and reached over, giving his hand the briefest touch. Now she knew why he came across as prickly at times, and why he didn't seem particularly friendly.

'You're at a new place,' she said quietly. 'A new hospital, with a whole group of people that don't know you, or anything about you. Surely you should just take some time to take a breath, and get to know everyone?' She paused, then added, 'And let them get to know you.'

Something was nagging at her. The way he'd spoken about his ex. He hadn't even said a name. Was he still thinking about her? Was he really up here because he didn't want to see her with her new fiancé? Was Jay Bannerman actually just on the rebound?

Anger flickered deep inside. She'd really enjoyed last night's kiss. Yes, she might have panicked for a second. But she'd sent him a text to let him know she was home and ended that with a kiss.

Skye had always struggled with relationships herself—mainly because she hadn't ever been inclined to give them the time and attention they probably deserved. She'd dated a lot. Meeting men was never a problem. But sooner or later, no matter how great the guy, they always got fed up with her devotion to work, and most relationships just petered out.

She blinked as she sat in front of Jay now. Did she even want a relationship with him?

He gave her a sad look. 'So, you're telling me to give Northern a chance?'

'I don't think people are talking about you, Jay. They have no reason to.'

He gave a slow nod. 'I guess.' Then his gaze met hers. 'Unless someone saw us last night?'

She froze. She literally froze. That hadn't even occurred to her. Of course, other hospital staff might have taken the same opportunity that they had, using the tickets to the show. It was always popular.

'It's just as likely no one saw us,' she countered, 'and if they did, you've only been here a few weeks, most people wouldn't recognise you.' She shook her head. 'There's no rumour to start.'

He gave a slow gulp. His head tilted slightly to the side. 'So, what about our kiss last night? What did that mean?'

Now she was on the spot. She would like it to mean something. But, on the other hand, what had really changed for her?

She was still entirely focused on her work. Was that likely to change any time in the future? No.

The kiss had made her feel special. It had made her feel connected. And whilst she hadn't felt that way in a long time, it didn't have to mean anything.

She met his gaze. 'I think we can put that down to a wonderful night out between friends. It ended the evening in a nice way.'

His eyebrows went up again. 'Nice?'

She gave a small smile, knowing he was pushing. 'Well, it wasn't exactly unpleasant,' she said, stringing the words out. 'But…' She straightened, trying to look a bit more serious. 'It's probably not a good idea for us. We work together. You're the supervisor of my research project. Things like that could become complicated. I don't want to be in a situation where either of us is uncomfortable working together.'

Now it was Jay's time to shift in his chair. 'Of course not,' he said quickly. 'Maybe we can just put it down to getting carried away with the Christmas spirit?'

Now she did laugh out loud. 'You?'

He pretended to look wounded, putting his hand to his chest. 'Yes, me. You think I can't be festive?'

She leaned across the table. 'Name Santa's reindeers.'

For a second he looked panicked. 'Rudolph,' he said triumphantly.

'There's eight more,' she replied, deadpan.

He shook his head. 'Give me something else.'

'Name five Christmas films.'

His brow furrowed and he concentrated. *'The Grinch,'* he said, almost wickedly—she'd called him that too.

'One.'

'*White Christmas.*' It was like he'd pulled that from the dregs of his mind.

'Two.' She drummed her fingers on the table, doing her best impression of being unimpressed.

'Eh...'

'Nope, I don't know a Christmas film called that.'

'Give me a moment.' He actually did look a bit worried, and that made her want to laugh out loud. After what seemed like the longest time, he let out a breath and frowned. 'I give up.'

She counted on her fingers. '*Santa Claus: The Movie, Miracle on Thirty-Fourth Street, Elf, The Polar Express, Last Christmas, The Christmas Chronicles, The Holiday, It's a Wonderful Life, Die Hard—*'

He cut her off. 'That is *not* a Christmas movie.'

She folded her arms. 'It is. And I'll fight to the death over that one.'

The tension between them appeared to have eased, because they both took long breaths.

He gave a resolute smile. 'So, Christmas spirit. Is that what we're going with?'

She wondered how he felt deep down. Because she wanted to say no. She wanted to tell him she was more than a little annoyed at getting kissed on the rebound by a handsome doctor with distracting brown eyes and a lilting accent.

If she was in some kind of Jane Austen adaptation, she would declare it terribly unfair.

But she wasn't, so she kept her expression impartial. 'I guess if we want to keep working together—well, it should be.'

He slid his hand across the table, and, for a brief second, she wondered if he was going to squeeze her hand, give her some kind of secret sign that this was just all nonsense.

But…his hand was in the position for shaking. So, she gripped his hand, probably just a little too tightly, and shook it. 'Agreed.'

He glanced over at the clock. 'Time to get back, you probably want to see Frank again.'

Frank. For about ten minutes she actually hadn't thought about him. That made her feel instantly guilty. Her chair scraped as she stood up quickly.

'Yes,' was her reply before she turned and left him to pick up their cups, and head back to the ward.

The next few days were hard on Skye. This was her time of year. And although her walk with Jay had been good, the kiss—and their conversation after—had left her feeling low.

She'd sat with Frank and his son Joe on and off for a few days until Frank had finally passed.

He'd been comfortable and had slipped away whilst both Joe and Skye had been in his room.

Skye had promised to help Joe with the funeral, and had given him a list of their fathers' mutual friends so he could start arrangements. It was only proper to help him. But it sparked a lot of old memories for her, and made her sad.

Her mum lived in Spain now, and had met someone last year. Skye was happy for her, because her mother had been sad and lonely when her father had died, and then for years afterwards. She'd lost her oomph for life, and this new man was only a couple of years older and was also a widower. He was good company for her mum, and Skye did approve. But it also meant it didn't feel appropriate to phone and be upset about all the memories of her father.

She was trying her best to keep things bright on the ward. But the last two nights she'd gone home and just hugged herself with a blanket on the sofa. Had that kiss unsettled her too? Her work ethic meant that she hadn't really dated any colleagues. She'd never really wanted to. But being alone wasn't always good. Being alone was just sometimes lonely. No wonder she wanted a dog or a cat.

The next morning, even though it wasn't even light yet, she found her most festive dress, bright red and decorated with tiny Santas, and a pair of knee-high black boots.

There were a few research meetings over the next week, and she needed to be prepared. More data was ready on the tumour samples, and she wanted to see how the AI had plotted them.

When she got to the ward it was barely seven o'clock. Indira was on the phone at the desk and she gestured Skye over.

'Why has the patient been down there so long? They could have come up to us at any point in the middle of the night?' Indira paused, then sighed and nodded. 'Send them straight up, our own doctor will deal with them.'

'What is it?' asked Skye as soon as Indira put down the phone.

'Renal cancer. Transfer in from a hospital in Ayrshire. We didn't receive the notification, and A&E have been slammed. The patient's been in there all night.'

'Oh no, poor soul,' said Skye. 'Are they sending them right up?'

Indira nodded. 'I'll get Ronnie to get the bed ready and find some breakfast for them.'

'I'll clerk them in.' Then she turned. 'Or, will we wait and see how they are? They might be knackered and need a sleep.'

Indira nodded. 'Thanks Skye.'

Skye hated when things like this happened. They shouldn't. But occasionally a referral would get lost—between ambulance transfers, messages not being passed on, consultants or GPs being on annual leave. It was rare, but it always made her feel terrible.

She liked to think the NHS offered a wonderful service. The thought of some poor patient—who was likely getting admitted because of worsening symptoms, or pain not being controlled—lying on an uncomfortable A&E trolley all night made her insides curl.

'What's wrong?' The deep voice was right at her shoulder.

She jumped. 'Where did you come from?' Then she frowned. 'And how do you know something is wrong?'

'I'm not blind. I can see the expression on your and Indira's faces. Is it something I should know about?'

She quickly explained. He looked around. 'It'll be breakfast time soon. Most of the porters will be delivering food trolleys.' He caught sight of Ronnie. 'How about Ronnie and I go down and pick the patient up?'

'You'd do that?' She was shocked. Most department heads wouldn't consider it their role to do something like that.

'Of course I will,' he replied and went to get Ronnie.

Fifteen minutes later the guys wheeled the trolley onto the ward and gently moved the patient over to their waiting bed.

Indira took a few moments to speak to the forty-year-old woman, who looked exhausted, and then came back with some tea and toast.

Jay met Skye at the nurse's station. 'Metastatic disease, she's tired, hungry and needs some pain relief. She also let me know she prefers female staff. Are you happy to take the lead?'

Skye took a few seconds to answer—she knew it had been two male staff who'd collected the woman from A&E.

'She was okay on the way up?'

He nodded. 'One of the female healthcare assistants came up with us.'

Skye nodded. 'Absolutely, I'll let her finish breakfast, sort out some pain relief and take it from there.'

She handed Jay another chart. 'I'll do you a trade. Leah's on her second day of chemo today and needs to be checked over later to see how she's tolerating it. Do you mind doing that?'

He gave a slow nod. There had been nearly a full two-week delay in her treatment because of her underlying infections. Those were now resolved, but they were both worried about her.

She ought to feel awkward around Jay because of their previous kiss. But with their conversation in the canteen—where she had been the one to insist that their kiss didn't have to mean anything deeper—a line had been firmly drawn in the sand. And since then, it hadn't been as awkward as she might have expected.

He was treating her just the same. But instead of feeling relief at having no tension at work, it was actually annoying her!

Had their kiss really meant nothing to him? She hated that she found herself occasionally staring at him, wondering what might have happened if they'd been in a different location, somewhere more private.

Maybe he spent his life just kissing girls? Because he was good at it. She had *never* been kissed like that, and that's what annoyed her the most.

It's what had been causing her dreams to sizzle over the last few days—it was proving very distracting. No matter how much she tried to push 'that' kiss into a box and lock it away, somehow it was sneakily managing to get itself back out.

She kept wondering what he made of all this.

Maybe she had misjudged the fact he was on the rebound. It certainly sounded like that, but annoyingly enough she couldn't see into his head, to see if that was how *he* actually felt.

The last thing she wanted to do was compromise their working relationship, but as much as she could tell, there was still a vibe in the air. She could feel it.

The ward was busy at this time of year. It was strange, but there always seemed to be a spate of people who received a cancer diagnosis just before Christmas. For the majority of people, even though the diagnosis was scary, they had a good chance of a cure. Jay was always honest with patients. Screening tests were invaluable, and often picked up a diagnosis before a person had a single symptom. Most people were grateful to be able to start treatment as soon as possible.

But Jay had just spent the last few days giving people diagnosis after diagnosis. It seemed like a revolving door. As a consultant oncologist he should be used to it, but even he was getting down.

As he stood as the nurses' station, he picked up a flyer about a drive-in Christmas movie experience, in Portobello, a coastal suburb of Edinburgh. That wasn't too far from him.

'Know what film they're showing?' he asked Indira.

She lifted her head and looked at the leaflet. 'They never tell you until you're actually there and parked up. Some people go, and hate what's been selected, others go, and find out it's their favourite Christmas film ever. I think there's a spoiler group about it online, but I don't know how reliable it is.'

She glanced down the corridor and smiled. 'You know who likes to go, don't you?'

He shook his head. 'No, who?'

Indira looked at him carefully. 'Skye. She loves it. I'm surprised she hasn't mentioned it already.'

He wasn't quite sure what to say. From Indira's gaze, it was like being under a microscope—he was sure she was watching for any sign of a facial twitch.

'I heard my name, what's going on?' asked Skye brightly.

Indira grinned. 'Jay was just saying that he'd like to go to the Christmas drive-in tonight.'

'He was?' Skye clearly couldn't hide the surprise on her face. 'And here was me thinking you didn't even know that many Christmas films,' she said under her breath.

Jay squirmed, but before he got a chance to

reply, Indira spoke again. 'And I was just saying how much you love that, and that you'd probably be going.'

Their eyes met. Both of them had the same deer-caught-in-headlights look, neither of them quite sure how to respond.

But Indira had already made her mind up about this. 'It starts at seven thirty, and it's popular. You'd both need to be there before seven.' She glanced at her watch, then turned to Jay. 'There are always food vans there, so you'll be able to grab some dinner. But you better go home and get changed first.' She carried on as if no one else was involved in this conversation. 'So, you'll pick up Skye about six-thirty then? Better get a move on you two.'

Skye's mouth was slightly open, as if she were trying to interrupt, but Indira locked her with a hard stare.

What could he say?

He had genuinely considered doing this tonight to try and lift his festive spirits a bit. Would it be so awkward to take Skye with him?

'I don't know Skye's address,' he murmured, glancing between both women.

Indira picked up a Post-it pad from the desk. 'Here you go,' she said, scribbling as she held Skye's gaze. 'It's easy to find.'

An awkward silence stretched out in front of them. Then Jay gave a brief nod of his head.

'Better get ready then,' he said, moving quickly down the corridor before Indira started dissecting him like a specimen.

By the time he pulled up outside Skye's, he wondered what on earth he was actually doing. He didn't want to have a relationship with a co-worker. It was clear Skye didn't want to have a relationship with him. He'd half expected her to text him with an excuse—he would have gladly taken it.

Skye's place was a semi-detached townhouse in a reasonable part of Edinburgh. The whole row of houses had different coloured front doors. Quirky, but also fun. There was a warm glow from her windows, which made him wonder what the inside was like.

It was good manners to go to the door but, before he had a chance, Skye opened her green front door and came out wearing a practically matching green coat. She had some things in her hand and blinked at his car.

He could have left it in storage back in London. But his father's old, red Alfa Romeo Spider had been his pride and joy, and it was in pristine condition. Most places that Jay took it someone offered to buy it.

Skye's eyes widened at the sight. 'Where did you get this?' she asked as she climbed inside.

'It was my father's. He restored it and loved it. When he moved to Brighton and said he wouldn't use it any more, I had it shipped over from Ireland.'

'You drove it up from London?'

He gave a short laugh. 'Did you think it wouldn't make it?'

She looked around the old-style dashboard, the convertible roof. 'Did it?'

He nodded. 'The engine is probably in better condition than most humans.' He waited a second and then twisted in his seat to face her. 'If this is too awkward, just say. I did mention to Indira that I was thinking about going, it was her who mentioned that you'd gone before.'

She raised her eyebrows. 'Haven't you realised yet that you don't argue with Indira?'

He let out a short laugh. 'I felt as if I was under some kind of microscope.'

'Me too,' she agreed, then looked at him carefully. 'We both know Christmas films aren't really your thing. Why did you want to go?'

He sighed. 'Honestly, I've been giving out diagnoses these last two days at an alarming rate. I just wanted something to distract me. To let me think about something else. It's been hard,' he admitted—not something he would usually do.

'People think we're made of granite or something,' she replied. 'Just because we chose oncology doesn't mean we won't have bad days like everyone else.'

She got it. She really did.

He nodded. 'I just wanted some kind of pick-me-up. Plus, you guilted me into it.'

'I what?' She was shaking her head.

'You shamed me,' he said matter-of-factly. 'You let me know that, if I get caught in some pub quiz, I only know the names of two Christmas films. It could be the difference between winning or losing.'

She gave him a smug smile. 'I'm glad that you take your pub quizzes seriously.'

Jay started the car and pulled out. If Skye didn't want to be here, then she wouldn't have come. He started towards Portobello.

'Did you eat?' she asked.

He shook his head. 'Indira said there are food vans.'

Skye pulled a face. 'I didn't really have a chance to warn you. It will be hotdogs, half-cooked burgers, chips and likely some kind of kebabs.' She pulled out her phone. 'But there is good news.'

'Tell me, please. From the description of the food, we'll both end up being referred to public health with some kind of gastro disaster.'

She turned her phone to face him, a genuine smile on her face. 'The film,' she said. 'It's *The Santa Clause.*'

He glanced sideways. Her eyes were shimmering. 'Is that a good one?'

'You've never heard of *The Santa Clause*?' her tone was incredulous.

He shook his head as he kept his eyes on the road. 'Should I have?'

She threw up her hands. 'Tim Allen. An ordinary guy hears a noise and goes outside to find Santa has fallen off his roof. He has to take over, and starts to turn in Santa. It's brilliant.'

'It is?' Jay wasn't convinced from the brief description.

But Skye settled back into her seat. 'If you're looking for some kind of pick-me-up, I guarantee you, this is it.'

'If you say so.'

They continued along the road, whilst Skye kept telling him parts of the story. The more she talked, the more enthusiastic she got. By the time they reached Portobello, they had to join a long line of cars to pay their entry fee and get in.

She nudged him with her elbow. 'See? This

is all because they've seen on the spoiler page what film it is tonight.'

'I'll take your word for it,' said Jay as he flashed his card at the machine. The barrier lifted.

'Park over here,' said Skye, directing him to a certain part of the drive-in, which was really just a large retail car park surrounded by warehouses. The screen was huge and rippling in the wind.

'Did you bring anything?' she asked as he slid his seatbelt off.

Jay felt momentarily panicked. 'No, how— what should I have brought?'

She held up the bag she had with her. 'Drinks, crisps, chocolate or, if you prefer fruit, I have tangerines.' She dangled the big string bag in front of his nose and he started to laugh.

'I've failed,' he said, then lent over her, accidentally brushing against her leg as he made a grab for the glove box. 'I might have some ancient mints in here.'

Even though it was dark in the car, he could still see the green of her eyes. Their gazes clashed and held for a moment.

He knew. He knew she'd felt the same buzz he had.

He leaned back into his own seat, but didn't

break their gaze. Skye licked her lips. He knew it was likely just a nervous reflex, but it sent his senses into overdrive.

'How about some chips?' he asked, hand grasping for the door handle.

She gave the tiniest of nods and he stepped out into the cold night air. Anything to cool his flushing skin.

He joined a snaking queue before realising he hadn't even asked if she wanted anything on hers. A quick executive decision was made to take one bag with salt and vinegar, and the other with salt and tomato sauce. He was happy with either, so would let her choose. He grabbed another couple of diet sodas and headed back to the car.

The screen had been playing adverts whilst the rest of the viewers had moved into their places around the car park. It was literally mobbed. He'd never seen anything like this before.

As he climbed back in, he suddenly realised that the Alfa might not be the best car in the world for this. The roof was in place, but it did let in a few drafts, and with the temperature due to drop to below zero it might be a cold watch.

'Salt and vinegar, or salt and sauce?' he asked as he pulled out his insulin pen and injected in his stomach.

'Tomato or brown sauce?' she queried.

He scoffed. 'Tomato. Who puts brown sauce on chips?'

'Me,' she answered as she took the bag with salt and vinegar.

As soon as they opened their bags the steam started fogging the windscreen. Jay started the engine again to clear the window.

'This car might not have been the best idea,' he admitted.

'Why?'

'Let's just say that, in a car this old, things can be a little draughty.'

She stared up at the roof above them and touched it with her hand. 'What's it made of?'

'Mohair.'

'What?' A deep furrow creased her brow. 'Are you serious?'

'Entirely. I'm just not sure it was expected to last this long.'

'It's rain proof?' She looked mildly panicked.

'I haven't got wet yet.'

Before she had a chance to say anything else the film started, sound booming from speakers at the front and sides of the car park.

It was odd. He'd never been to a drive-in before. The screen was big enough to see easily, and he could see cars filled with multiple people around them.

'How long is it going to take to get out of here?' he asked.

Skye took a quick glance around the large car park. 'Probably about an hour. But don't worry. I'll teach you about other films whilst we're waiting.'

The film was surprisingly good, but the temperature in the car was plummeting fast. After half an hour, Skye gave a sniff and pulled her coat further around himself. She'd already told him to put his engine off, in case it drained the car battery, and the truth was he couldn't remember the last time he'd renewed the battery.

'There's an age-old way to keep warm,' he said quietly.

'What's that?'

'Body heat.'

She stared at him. 'I can't believe you just said that.'

'Are you cold, or are you cold?'

'I'm cold,' she admitted.

'And if we were stuck in the Antarctic somewhere, would you worry about getting body heat from someone you don't really like?'

'We're in Portobello,' she bit back. 'And I didn't say I don't like you.'

He gave her a smile and held out his arm. 'Then keep warm.'

Her jaw was slightly clenched, and he wondered if she wanted to get into a fight about it. But, after a few seconds, he could see her relent, before she shifted slightly in her seat and let her body press against his.

Okay, so it wasn't ideal. The car made things a little awkward. And it wasn't the optimum way to keep warm, but it was better than nothing.

'You should have a blanket,' she scolded. 'What if you got caught at the side of the road in a snowstorm?'

'I don't take her out in the snow,' he said quickly.

'Her?' She turned to face him.

He shrugged. 'Miriam.'

'You called your car Miriam?'

He was conscious how close they were. How he could intermittently see tiny freckles on her nose, depending on the way the light reflected from the film screen.

'My dad called his car Miriam,' he replied, 'and I have absolutely no idea why.'

She seemed to pause, just staring at him for a bit, and he wondered if he'd managed to get tomato sauce on his face.

'What?' he asked.

After last time around, no matter how much he was tempted to lean in and kiss her, he wouldn't. Not after she'd left so quickly. And not after their conversation where she'd made it clear she wasn't interested.

His curiosity was piqued. 'So, you don't—*not* like me then?'

She gave him a hard stare, but didn't make any attempt to put any distance between them. Heat was starting to spread.

She blinked. 'I think you're okay.'

'Okay?' He couldn't help but smile again. 'As in, okay to work with, okay to talk to if there's no one else around, or okay to consider if he were the last man standing?'

The edges of her lips crept upwards. 'All of the above.'

He let his head flop back. 'I'm going to die of happiness from the compliments tonight.'

Her gaze narrowed slightly and he sensed her stiffen. 'I'm not anyone's rebound girl.'

Now it was his turn to stiffen. 'Why on earth would you think that?'

'From what you said the other day in the canteen. You know that you're prickly and push people away. You also told me that you wanted to get away from watching your ex celebrate her new engagement. You're clearly on the rebound.'

He shook his head in bewilderment. 'If I was on the rebound, I'd still have feelings towards my ex. I don't. I'm just not entirely sure that workplace romances are the best thing.'

'You think that because you're still hurting,' she insisted.

Jay could feel his hackles rising. 'I think that because—like I explained to you—I don't like being the subject of gossip at work.'

She just stared at him, as though she didn't really believe what he was saying.

'Let me give you an example. I've been here— what, three weeks? I barely know anyone at the Great Northern. But, in the last few days, I've heard gossip about the potential father of Poppy Evans' baby, I've heard others talking about a guy called Max, and taking bets on when he might lighten up, and if some other female doctor might be the person that's affecting him. Do you know her? Tamsin O'Neill? And I've heard rumours about a maybe affair between one of the radiographers and his secretary.'

He shook his head. 'It's intrusive, and potentially harmful. But hospitals are notorious for gossip. I just don't want to be part of it.' He waited a second as she continued to stare. 'And none of that—*none* of that—means I'm still in love with my ex. I actually wonder if I was ever in love with her in the first place.'

She shifted, her body, which had been aligned with his, moving back to her own seat.

All of a sudden, the space seemed immense.

'Let's just watch the film,' she said.

There was really no arguing with that. He settled back in his own seat, frustrated, and wondering where on earth those thoughts had come from.

After a few long minutes Skye reached into her bag and brought out a cardboard box of chocolates. She opened the box, took the first one, then handed it wordlessly to him.

The box passed back and forward between them for the next half hour until the film ended.

He gathered up their rubbish and took it to the nearest bin, relieved when he got back in the car and it started with no issues.

As he got back in, he caught the aroma of her perfume again—his heart rate quickened. She was still having a crazy effect on him.

How could he blame her for getting the wrong end of the stick when his brain told him one thing, and his body another?

His heart sank as he looked at the queue ahead. Skye had been entirely right. This would take an hour at least to get out of the venue.

They exchanged glances and she gave a conciliatory smile. 'Truce?' she asked.

'Truce,' he agreed, feeling a wave of relief. They really didn't need for things to be awkward between them.

'Great,' she said as she sagged back in the seat. 'Now, which Christmas film do you want to see next?'

CHAPTER SIX

SKYE LOOKED AT the piles of notes on the table on her desk. In days gone by, it hadn't been unusual for patients to have three or four volumes of ancient paper files with their medical history enclosed. In a lot of cases, these had been scanned and converted to a digital system. But sometimes the scanning process hadn't been accurate. And if a patient had previously lived in a different area, chances were their notes were still on paper. Which is why her desk was currently deluged.

Jay hadn't been joking about the sharp rise in diagnoses recently. All of these people who'd had tumours biopsied were potential candidates for her research project.

But, like any research project, there were a strict range of parameters for any patient being allowed to have their data examined by the AI programme. And those parameters meant an extensive deep dive into their past history to ensure they didn't have anything to exclude them from the project. It wasn't just time consuming, it was exhausting. And Skye didn't want to ask anyone to assist in this process, because one mistake, one tiny detail missed, could affect the impact and reliability of the whole study.

It was making her antsy. Just like working alongside Jay on a daily basis.

Since their Christmas drive-in—which Indira had asked them both about—it had almost felt as if she was walking on tiptoes around him.

He'd clearly been unhappy with her suggestion he was on the rebound. And she'd fixed that idea in her head so much she hadn't really considered other possibilities.

Maybe this was partly her fault. Her previous relationships hadn't really been a success, with any partner—whether or not they worked in her hospital. All of the guys she'd dated had eventually got fed up with placing second to her work. So maybe she was actually trying to scupper this one before it could even start?

It was easier to blame him, and feel offended, than look at herself.

And the more she thought about it, the more a little flame flickered inside her. Jay Bannerman was *not* on the rebound. If she'd hadn't run off that night at the market, could their relationship have started to blossom further?

In the car the other night she'd still felt that sizzle, that heat. Neither of them had acted on it. But deep down, apart from Indira's organising, she'd wanted to go with him. If she hadn't, she could have made an excuse at any point. But the fact was, she did want to spend time in Jay's company. What could that even mean now?

She pushed the files aside, knowing she needed maximum concentration when she was looking at them. She didn't want to risk missing anything.

Leah was still on the ward, as was their new patient, Kelly Robertson, the forty-year-old with metastatic cancer. Skye decided to review them both.

'How you doing, Leah?' she asked as she entered her room.

Leah's colour was looking rosier, and she'd been eating better the last few days. She looked up from the book she was reading. 'Sorry, what?'

Skye laughed as she sat down. 'Am I disturbing you? What are you reading?'

Leah held up the hardback book. '*Thursday Murder Club.* Dr Bannerman brought it in for me. He says he has all four if I like them.'

Skye was a little shocked. 'Jay gave you that?'

Leah smiled and nodded. 'Apparently he reads like a fiend.'

She started to get curious. 'And what do you think of it?'

Leah held it to her chest. 'I love it. It's great. Just what I need.' It was actually the happiest Skye had seen her since she'd been admitted. And it was lovely to see—Leah had had a tricky start to her treatment, and it was nice to see things settling down.

Skye could see she was almost three-quarters of the way through the book.

'I had no idea Dr Bannerman was a reader.' Skye smiled. 'Maybe you should give it to me when you've finished, and I'll give it a try.'

Leah gave a calculated look at the book. 'I'll be finished in another hour.'

Skye asked her another few questions about her treatment, her symptoms and her pain relief, making a few minor tweaks to her plan, before carrying on down the corridor.

Kelly took a bit longer to assess. Hers was a slow-growing cancer, which had spread, but was actually still at a manageable stage. Once they had her pain completely under control, she would be able to go home.

When she was finished she headed into Jay's

office. He was behind his desk eating some chocolate.

'You okay?' she asked straight away, the alarm sounding on his phone.

'I will be in five minutes,' he said, silencing the alarm. She noted he was eating the chocolate from the advent calendar, which was actually really small.

'How about I go and get you a coffee and a chocolate digestive from the secret stash in my desk?'

He stared for a moment, and she wondered if he was going to argue. But he pulled out his own pack of digestives from his drawer. 'Actually, I'd love a coffee.'

She brought it back five minutes later and sat down with her notes. 'Okay to talk about some patients?'

He nodded.

She ran over the minor changes she'd made for Leah, and the plan she had for Kelly. Jay, in turn, talked about two of the older patients in the ward, both with breast cancer, but both managing well. Neither of them were steady on their feet, and with their cancer treatment there was always a risk of osteoporosis, which could lead to broken bones. The physiotherapist and occupational therapist were assessing them both.

'I didn't know you were a reader,' said Skye with a tinge of amusement.

He arched one brow. 'Who gave away my secret?'

'Leah. She's a teenager, what do you expect? Plus, she's loving that book you gave her.'

His face brightened. 'Great,' he slid his arm under the desk and came out holding a blue-trimmed book, 'I brought her the second. I knew she would love it.'

'I might have to read these,' said Skye, her fingers brushing against his as she took the book, flipping it over to read the back. 'What else do you read?'

'Mainly crime, a little sci-fi at times and any non-fiction that involves shipwrecks or Antarctica.' He watched her eyes skimming the blurb at the back of the book. 'Do you read?'

Skye sat back in her chair and crossed her legs. She noticed him watching her legs as she did it, and it gave her an illicit thrill. The ward was quiet now—most people had gone home. Could they engage in some harmless flirting again?

'Do I read? I'm never happier than spending a day in one of Edinburgh's many brilliant bookshops. I especially like shops with those moveable ladders. You know the ones? It's on the ambition list with the dogs.'

He sat back and gave her an amused glance. 'Well, I didn't see inside your house, but you must have one of those large front rooms. Surely you could put one of those bookcases there?'

She pulled a face. 'Old house. The floors are a bit uneven, and the wall is not exactly square. I would need to get someone to custom build for me, and in Edinburgh that's very expensive.'

He blew out a long, slow breath. 'I can only imagine.' Then he leaned forward with a glint in his eye. 'The place I've got has built-in book shelves.'

She scowled at him. 'You'd better be joking.'

He leaned back and stretched out his legs. 'Nope.'

'I'm beginning to regret making you a coffee now.'

He stretched out his arms. 'It's getting late, why haven't you gone home?'

'Why haven't you?'

He shot her a glance. 'What is this, tit for tat?'

She leaned forward, speaking in a low voice. 'And why would you think that?'

She was watching his eyes again, and this time they went straight to her cleavage. Skye never really wore anything revealing at work.

Her red wraparound dress covered all the parts of her it should, but when she'd leaned forward, he might have had the opportunity to catch a glimpse of the now deep V at her neckline.

As his gaze lifted, their eyes met. She held that gaze. Not looking away. Jay didn't seem embarrassed to have been caught looking, instead the edges of his lips turned upwards. His voice was low, almost a whisper. 'Seems when you work later, you can get distracted.'

She toyed with the gold necklace around her throat, knowing that those actions would taunt him. He shifted slightly in his chair, and that made her smile.

'So, today's lesson is that you're a book lover,' she said. 'As well as the old news that you're a Christmas film virgin.'

'I'll have you know that I take my lessons seriously. I've watched *Die Hard*, *Home Alone* and *Bad Santa*.'

'The list is much bigger than that.'

He shrugged. 'I know, but I've got to start somewhere.'

She straightened up, letting her back arch. 'Why don't you come and help me with the research? I've got a dozen files to read, and two sets of eyes are better than one.'

He paused for a moment before standing up,

a little closer than normal. She could practically feel the heat from his body.

'Is there a reward?' he asked, his voice huskier than she expected. It sent a shot up her spine. Those brown eyes of his were enveloping, like some kind of treacle, just trying to pull her in. She could easily get lost.

She licked her lips. 'There could be.' She spun around and walked out of his office, swinging her hips a little more than necessary.

He was right on her heels. As he walked into her office he closed the door behind them.

She let her finger drag on the desk as she pulled up a chair next to hers. 'Be my guest.'

'Is this the part where we sing?' he joked.

'I don't think I can quite manage Angela Lansbury,' she replied as she sat down, letting her wrap dress naturally position itself. She didn't adjust it to hide the way it revealed part of her thighs.

He sat down next to her, his leg brushing against hers, then frowned when he saw the packed files on the desk. 'You weren't joking. What are all these?'

She sighed. 'The patient files that aren't digital. I need to go through them to make sure all patient histories are declared before they join the study.'

He put his elbow on the desk, leaning closer to her. 'You're doing this yourself?'

She leaned towards him. 'Well, who else would do it?'

His muscles tensed around his neck. 'Why wouldn't you get a research assistant or some admin help you?'

He was so close—she inhaled his woody aftershave. The top button of his shirt was unfastened and she could see some tiny dark hairs at the base of his throat. Her fingers wanted to reach out and touch them.

But he'd asked a question he expected her to answer. She tugged down the clip that had been holding up her hair. Her dark curls fell around her shoulders. 'I won't have this study compromised. If I miss something, then it's my fault. But I won't miss anything, so that's why I do it myself.'

He looked a touch annoyed. 'But why would you want to spend hours doing this, when your time could be better spent on other parts of the study?'

She twisted a bit of her hair around one finger. 'These are the things that compromise a study. Something missed, which is then discovered way down the line. That Patient One Forty-Four had a strong family history of cancer, which could have meant a genetic component was involved. That Patient Seventy-Six was given an experimental vaccine as part of another study thirty years ago, which they'd subsequently forgotten about.'

She took a deep breath and looked him in the eye. 'Attention to detail is important.' She gave a hint of a smile. 'You should know that.'

She let those words hang in the air between them. Jay reached up and took a tress of her hair, winding it around his own finger in slow motion. He gave it the lightest tug and she moved her face closer to his.

'But not all the details have to be yours,' he said, his warm breath close to her cheek.

'I'm a control freak,' she said hoarsely. 'I think you should know that.'

His lips were only inches from hers. She could almost taste them.

He gave a smile. 'I think I can live with that.' His voice was a whisper, pulling her in further.

This time when their lips met there were no spectators. They were behind a closed door in a ward with minimal staff. Her hands wrapped around his shoulders and back, and his mouth moved quickly, from her lips down to her throat.

That connection took her breath away. That

feel of his slight stubble against her soft skin made her want to grab him and not let go.

She let out a soft moan as his jawline scraped the base of her throat. He moved closer, then kissed up the other side of her neck to her ear, moving back to her lips.

Even though his mouth was on hers, he was too far away. She shifted, moving from her chair onto his lap. Heat emanated through his shirt to her hands. She toyed with the top buttons.

Her head really wasn't on work right now, although in the background a voice was whispering words of warning. She started to undo those buttons so she could place her hands directly on his warm chest.

It was Jay's turn to shift now and let out a little groan. But he didn't stop kissing her. He kept going. The guy should get awards for this. She didn't want to know where he had practised, she just wanted him to keep focused on her.

Her hands ran through his hair. It was already tousled, but she liked the fact it was little longer than normal—it gave her something to grab hold of.

Her wrap dress was moving. The soft jersey gave way easily to Jay's hands as they slid around her breast.

She was losing focus and concentration and she pushed herself harder against him.

There was a soft knock at the door. 'Skye? Are you still here?'

They froze. Like cartoon characters, eyes wide, mouths open. It must only have been a millisecond, but it felt too long.

Skye jumped up and pushed her dress back into place. Thankfully the soft jersey obliged. She had no idea what she'd done with her hair clasp, or what she actually looked like. She took a few strides towards the door in the hope of intercepting anyone who might want to get in, giving Jay a few more seconds to fix his shirt.

She pulled the door open. Soo Yun was a Korean medical student who worked part time in medical records to supplement her studies. She had a pile of notes in her hands and was struggling with them.

'I've got the rest of the files you requested for your study.' She smiled.

'Fantastic,' said Skye, standing back with the door wide open, making room for Soo Yun. They'd talked about the study on a number of occasions and Soo Yun was genuinely interested.

As she spun around, Jay was sitting behind the desk, his head leaning on his hand in the most casual way.

'More files?' He smiled. His shirt was intact, and his hair actually looked less rumpled than normal.

Skye had a ten-second panic. Was her make-up halfway across her face? Did she look dishevelled? But Soo Yun hadn't reacted in any way when she'd opened the door. And by now Jay was on his feet, taking half the notes and making space on the desk for them.

'Next time bring a trolley.' He smiled at Soo Yun. 'Don't want to hurt your back with all those files.'

'I weight-lift,' she said matter-of-factly as she slid the rest of the pile on the desk. 'They're not heavy, just...' she stared at the wonky pile '...uneven.'

'Thanks so much,' said Skye. 'This should be the last for a while.'

Soo Yun gave a nod and waved her hand as she headed to the door. 'Let me know if you need any help.'

She disappeared back into the corridor as Skye tried to catch her breath.

As she looked up at Jay, he started laughing. It was infectious. She started laughing too.

She leaned back against the wall, hand on her heart. 'Oh my, can you imagine if we'd been caught?'

He walked over, just inches away. 'Maybe not ideal,' he agreed. He licked his lips and paused a few moments. 'Shall we call it a night?'

'Yes.' The word was out quicker than she really wanted it to be, and he gave the merest flinch.

'See you tomorrow.' His voice sounded casual, but she wondered if she'd just offended him for the second time.

Two strikes and you're out, a little voice said in her head.

Hers was the last office in the row. There was no hospital room opposite and no one in the corridor outside.

She leaned forward and brushed the briefest kiss on his cheek. 'See you tomorrow.'

She sat back behind her desk. By the time she looked up, Jay was already gone.

CHAPTER SEVEN

HIS EYES FLICKERED OPEN. He hadn't shut his blinds completely and he could see the sun struggling to rise in the deep purple sky outside, giving the horizon a strange glow.

It was Saturday. He had no on-call. And he knew that Skye was off too.

He reached over and grabbed his phone, scrolling social media for a whole ten seconds before he pulled up his contacts.

Skye Campbell was in there. Was it too early to text? She struck him as an early riser, but he could be wrong.

He still hadn't had a chance to buy a Christmas tree for his place. He still had some stuff down in London, and was merely renting out his place right now. But he wasn't such a Grinch that he didn't at least put something up for Christmas.

He wouldn't buy a real one. Mainly because he wouldn't know where to go. But there were a few other things he wanted to pick up today. Before he gave himself time to reconsider, he sent a text.

Do you have plans?

His reply came within a few seconds.

What did you have in mind?

Then a few moments later:

Don't tell me someone's phoned in sick at work?

He laughed.

No. No work issues. But wanting to get a few things for Christmas and see a few sights. Want to join me?

After another few moments, he realised he was holding his breath waiting for a reply. He could see the little dots on the screen. How much was she typing?

Since you're awake, I know a place that does a great breakfast. As long as your Christmas shopping will allow me to introduce you to Edinburgh's best bookshops, I'm in. There's also a Christmas brass band concert in Princes Street

Gardens. Bring your walking shoes and some warm clothes!

She sent him a pin on a map—obviously the place she wanted to go for breakfast.

Thirty minutes?

He couldn't reply quickly enough. Thirty minutes later he was in a quirky café on Leith Walk. He found a table and Skye appeared, wearing a bright pink coat and a grey hat with flaps over her ears. She had sturdy boots on, and took off her jacket to reveal jeans and a jumper.

'Did you know I love Christmas shopping?' She smiled as she sat down.

'I guessed you might. Plus, I need some help,' he conceded.

She gave a wave to the guy behind the counter. 'Do you know what you want?'

'Haven't even looked.'

'Do you trust me?' Her green eyes were dancing with mischief. It was a good start.

'I may live to regret this, but go on.'

She beamed. 'Aldo, can I just have my usual, times two?'

Ten minutes later, two plates of toast with scrambled egg and bacon, and two skinny lattes appeared.

She lifted her knife and fork and then paused. 'Okay for your diabetes?'

'Absolutely,' he said, checking his phone, then taking out his insulin pen and injecting.

She wrinkled her nose. 'Aren't you supposed to do that a bit before you eat? Sorry, I should have told you what I'd ordered.'

He shook his head. 'Everyone is different. For me, the fast-acting insulin works *fast*. It was a bit of nightmare when I was a junior doctor and carrying a page. I learned to always order something I could eat on the move, because if I'd already jagged, then sat down to eat and page went off…' He was still smiling as he let his voice drift off.

'Ooh,' she said as she pulled a face.

'Right.'

They ate leisurely as she queried his shopping list.

'I need a tree, but we'll probably have to buy that last.'

'Not really, we can buy from somewhere that will deliver. They probably won't do it till the end of the day.'

'Okay,' he said as he sipped his coffee. 'Then, I'm absolutely up for the bookshops. I always buy my sister and my mum and dad books. And I'll buy them some other things to go alongside.'

'Anything in particular?'

He turned over his phone and showed Skye a picture of his sister. 'She has quite similar taste to you in clothes. Probably a jumper or a shirt? My mum likes jewellery, so if there are any places with quirky jewellery I'm sure I'll find her something.'

'And your dad?'

There was the tiniest difference in tone when she asked the question. He reached and put his hand over hers.

'Sorry, you don't need to help me pick something for my dad.'

She shook her head, and her expression was genuine. 'No, it's fine. Honestly. It's actually kind of nice. I can't pick something for my dad, but I'm happy to help you find something for yours.'

Jay watched her carefully. 'Okay,' he agreed. 'Well, my dad likes art. Not fancy art. But genuine hand-painted stuff. So, if there are any arts and crafts shops around, probably something from there?'

She smiled. 'Some of the bookshops we'll visit also sell art. One has kind of Scottish landscapes, and the other has more cats and dogs kind of stuff.'

He looked at her coat. 'How many coats do

you actually have? I don't think I've seen you wear the same one twice.'

She sat back proudly. 'I have coats in many colours, and lots of leopard, zebra and snake prints too. I've bought them over the years, and just take care of them. I love a good coat.'

He pointed. 'Hats and scarves too?'

'And gloves. There are never enough gloves in the world.'

'Well then, let's get started.' Jay paid the bill and they left the café together.

'Know what I like best about this café?'

He frowned. 'Apart from the good breakfast?'

She nudged him. 'It's literally fifty feet away from a bookshop—' she paused for effect '—with ladders.'

The expression on her face made a surge of warmth spread through him. He really enjoyed being in her company. She could easily have said no today. And whilst he was sure he could have searched the city to find what he needed, it was so much better doing it with a friend.

They spent the next hour in the bookshop. It was on multiple levels, with shelves up to the ceilings, so the ladders were essential. Skye spent quite a bit of time in the fantasy section, and Jay found a new release from his favourite crime author. He also found a cosy crime for his mum, and a dark historical that was right up his sister's alley.

Skye came over and looked at what he'd picked.

'Interesting,' she said, putting the latest Tik-Tok sensation on the counter at the till. 'What about your dad?'

Jay gave another glance over his shoulder. 'Truth is my dad loves Irish fiction, but he's read most of it. He's started to read some Australian crime authors and is really enjoying them. So, I'll see if I can find him something along those lines.'

'Is it the authors he likes or the setting?'

'Oh, definitely the setting. Anything set in the outback, far away from civilisation, that's his thing.'

'I'm sure we'll find something.'

After they'd paid for their books, Skye took him to a department store, where he ordered a medium-sized pre-lit tree and some decorations that could be delivered later that day. Then she took him down some side streets, and they found a few craft shops with jewellery, before he picked a necklace in a waterfall design with abalone shell, and a matching pair of earrings.

There were also a few boutiques and they browsed through them. Skye disappeared to try a green jumper dress, which matched her eyes—and hugged all her curves—and Jay found a similar one in violet that he was sure his sister would love. He paid for them both as she was getting changed again. When she went to the till, the assistant smiled, folded the dress, wrapped it in tissue and put it in a paper bag, before refusing payment and nodding at Jay.

She came over with her eyes shining, holding up her bag. 'You bought me this?'

'Of course, you looked fabulous.'

She tilted her head to the side a little. 'But what if I hadn't liked it?'

He gave her a nonchalant look. 'Then my sister would have got two.'

He could tell from the moment she'd caught sight of her reflection in the dress that she'd loved it. And she'd looked fantastic. He hadn't been able to resist buying it for her.

She gave him a shy kind of smile. 'Thank you,' she said, accepting the bag he offered.

'Lunch?' she asked. 'There's an Italian pizza place around the corner?'

He nodded.

They had a relaxed lunch with some wine, before heading out into the cold Edinburgh air again.

The city had got much busier. The streets were

full of people who were obviously on tours, and those who were on day trips to the theatre.

'You wanted to sightsee?' she said, a crafty tone in her voice.

'Oh, no, but what do you have in mind?' he asked.

'Is your blood sugar okay?'

'Why?'

She'd slipped her arm into his as they'd threaded through the streets, but now she stopped and looked upwards. 'Because the best view in Edinburgh is up there.'

Jay looked up. 'We're going to climb the Scott Monument?'

The tall gothic monument was close to the train station, and towered over the main street in Edinburgh. Jay knew it was a tribute to the Scottish author Sir Walter Scott.

'Just as long your blood sugar can take it,' she smiled.

He looked up again. 'Of course I can.'

Two hundred and eighty-seven steps later— spotting different statues all the way up—they were on the highest viewing platform with a panoramic view of the city. The breeze was more than a little brisk, and he pulled his hat from his pocket, tugging it down over his hair.

'Wow,' he said as Skye started to point out

different parts of the city to him. The view was truly amazing, but even on a cold and windy day like this, the monument was busy. It wasn't long before they had to climb back down the spiral stairs to reach the bottom.

'We're in the perfect place now,' Skye declared.

'Why?'

'Because we're right next to Princes Street Gardens, and the brass band is playing next to the fountain.'

They made their way down to the gardens, which were full of people and multiple refreshment stalls. They bought some coffee and a muffin for Skye, then made their way to where the brass band was set up. The band members ranged in age from young kids and teenagers to adults and pensioners, all wearing gold-buttoned black jackets with matching hats. Another part of the gardens was set up as a Winter Wonderland, with an ice rink and a Ferris wheel, but they settled in with the rest of the crowd to listen to the brass band.

Even though it was cold, the atmosphere in the gardens was warm. People were there to enjoy themselves. Families, couples and groups of friends, all with smiles on their faces, surrounded them.

The band started with some Christmas carols, which most of the crowd sang along to, before moving to some more modern Christmas tunes. That had people raising their voices even louder as they all sang along to 'Last Christmas' and 'Fairytale of New York', albeit very out of tune.

As Jay watched those around him, he was struck by how happy he actually was to be there. And part of that was down to who he was with. He'd spent so much time in his head, vowing he would never have another relationship with a colleague, but here he was, with a colleague, and all could think about was what had happened in her office, and what might have happened next.

Skye Campbell wasn't Jessica, his ex-fiancée. Now that he could look back with clearer vision, he could see the faults in their relationship. But that also made him wary. Both he and Jessica had been completely devoted to their work. Much like he still was now, and much like the traits he also admired in Skye. But how much time could two doctors—devoted to their work—actually give to each other? Maybe he was a fool for actually considering things in his head again.

But somehow, he just couldn't stop thinking about her. He could see people around them giving occasional glances. Making assumptions.

And he wasn't sorry. If he met anyone from the hospital now, he wouldn't try and hide the fact they were there together. He was happy to be there with her. No, he was proud to be there with her.

Skye threw her head back to try and reach the last note of 'Merry Xmas Everybody' and he winced, then laughed. Okay, maybe not proud of the singing. It was entirely in its own key.

She slapped his arm, her face lighting up. 'Are you laughing at my singing?'

He slid an arm around her waist. 'I think the whole of the gardens is laughing at your singing,' he joked.

She leaned towards him. 'Feeling festive yet, Dr Grumpy?'

He looked down at the bags at their feet, and at the people around them. It had started to get a bit darker and the lights in the gardens had come on.

'I'm definitely feeling something,' he admitted.

She glanced down at the paper programme someone had passed them. 'Only two songs to go.'

'How about some dinner before we finish?'

She gave a small smile, her hands resting on his other arm. 'Sure.'

* * *

Skye was having the best day. From the moment she'd received his text this morning, her heart had been jumping.

She couldn't quite put her finger on what was so perfect about all of this. Was it the fact she knew she'd brought a genuine smile to the face of the guy who'd been nicknamed Dr Grumpy? Or was it just the fact she was getting to know him more and more, and liked everything she found out?

From breakfast, to shopping, to sightseeing and lunch, her day had been just perfect. Jay Bannerman was good company, whether he meant to be or not.

She could easily have bought her own dress—and would have—but it had been a nice gesture on his part that he'd paid for it.

If she'd been on her own today, what would she have done? Much the same as this, but she wouldn't have had someone to share it with. She was an independent woman and liked her own space, but sometimes it was nice to have someone at your side. Whether it was merely friendship, or something else, she wasn't entirely sure.

The other night at work they could easily have ended up as friends with benefits if they hadn't been interrupted. But in a way she was glad they had been. First, she would hate to be caught in a compromising position at work. Second, she really wasn't a friends-with-benefits kind of girl. She might not be particularly good at relationships, but she wasn't really casual either. It struck her that maybe she just hadn't met the right person yet. Or maybe she had and had been too focused on work, letting them slip through her fingers.

But no one had really given her the buzz that Jay did. As soon as he started talking, she practically swayed to the tune of his voice. It was magical. Not that she'd let him know that.

No one had lit a fire in her belly when she'd been kissed the way Jay had. When his hands had slid inside her dress...

She shivered, and felt him pull her against him. The gardens were cold, but the brass band were great and as they played their final song, she was almost sad they were finished—even if she couldn't feel her toes any more.

'Anything in particular you'd like for dinner?' she asked him.

He held out his hands. 'I'm easy. You've done good at picking so far. So just pick some place that you like.'

Skye put her hands on her hips and thought for a moment. 'What I really want is a cocktail,' she admitted, then something came to mind and she clicked her fingers, pointing at Jay.

'You've still to get something for your dad, and there's a Scottish restaurant down one of the side streets, near some small shops that have some paintings in them.' She glanced at her watch. 'It's only five o'clock—the shops stay open to eight on a Christmas Saturday night in Edinburgh, and the restaurants won't be busy yet, so we should be fine.'

Jay gathered up the bags at their feet. 'Lead the way.'

It took around ten minutes for the crowds to file out of the gardens. Lots of them were heading in the direction of the ice rink and Ferris wheel, but thankfully Skye and Jay were going in the opposite direction.

As they bustled through the people, Skye reached out and grabbed his hand, keeping them together when people unexpectedly stopped in front of them, gathered in crowds or slowed to admire some lights or a view.

They ducked down the smaller street, which instantly felt as if it were in a different century. Shop windows weren't wide panes, but more small squares that were slightly bevelled as if they had been there for ever.

Skye pointed to a wooden sign hanging far in front. 'There's the restaurant, but there're a few shops here that might suit.' She directed him to a craft shop, the stone shopfront painted in cream and brown, several items on display in the window. Jay looked for a second, then gestured he wanted to go inside.

It was one of those kinds of shops that, when two people were in it, felt easily crowded. They kept their elbows tucked in as they admired the glass cabinets and pictures on the walls. Some were paintings, some were sketches. There were golf courses, a few of Edinburgh Castle at different points in history, a few street scenes, and some darker ones that matched some of the history of Edinburgh.

The man behind the counter gave them a smile as he continued reading his paper. 'If you need any help, just ask.'

Jay was glad. There was nothing worse that someone hanging over your shoulder, remarking on everything that fell into your line of sight.

'I've found my favourite,' whispered Skye.

'Where?' Jay scanned the walls, trying to think what one she might pick.

She nudged him and pointed down near the floor. He bent down and picked up the small, framed sketch. He turned it one way, then the other.

'Is that a blue dinosaur?' He was totally confused.

She was still grinning. 'Looks like it.'

He glanced at her. 'But dinosaurs weren't blue.'

'Prove it.' She kept smiling. 'It's not like any of us have seen them.'

'What even is it?' he whispered back.

'When I was at school, we called them a diplodocus, but I think the proper name is something else.' She gave a shrug. 'Or I might be mixed up.'

Jay held it closer. He could see the fine lines of varying depth. The drawing was meticulous, and he wondered where on earth the artist had been inspired.

'This is your favourite?' he asked again.

She nodded without shame. 'Absolutely. The hint of blue just gives it an edge. Makes it that bit different.'

'A blue dinosaur?' he asked again, shaking his head. He really wanted to start laughing.

'Maybe not for your dad,' she said as she continued around the small space. 'What about this one?'

He moved next to her. This was a painting of

Edinburgh Castle. It was set a few hundred years ago. The castle looked damp, dirty and tired. It was nightfall and little pockets of light—clearly where fires had been lit—gave the painting an unusual glow. There was something quite mesmerising about it.

'Has he ever been to Edinburgh?' she asked.

He nodded. 'A few times. He had a placement in Edinburgh during his training.'

'His training?'

He gave an ironic smile. 'My dad's a doctor. At least he was—he retired a few years ago.'

'What kind of doctor was he?'

'A GP. He loved it, but I remember him getting called out at all times of the day or night. He worked incredible hours—and didn't think anything of it.'

'So, you're glad he retired?'

'Absolutely. He and my mum bought a camper and have been halfway around Europe, getting into all sorts of trouble.'

'Really?'

'Oh really. My dad thinks his accent will literally let him get away with anything.'

'And does it?'

Jay pulled a face. 'Mainly. I think it's safe to say my dad's blessed with the Irish charm.' And before she got a chance to say anything, he added, 'You know, the thing I forgot to pick up on my way out the door?'

She laughed and put her hand on his arm. 'Don't worry, you're starting to heat up. Maybe someone sent it in the post for you to pick up.'

'What? I'm not Dr Grumpy anymore?'

He held the painting under one of lights in the shop to get a better view. Skye looked at him carefully, a small smile on her lips.

'You're getting better,' she said in a voice that sent a lightning bolt down his spine.

Their eyes connected. 'And what does that mean?'

She smiled, as if she were thinking of something all to herself, before looking up again. 'It means, we'll see.'

The owner was staring at them now, so Jay paid for the painting, with delivery promised for tomorrow, before they headed back out into the street, towards the restaurant.

As she threaded her arm through his, his brain was asking the obvious question. What did he really have against a relationship with a colleague? One bad experience was just that—one bad experience. Did it mean he had to shut himself away from other opportunities when they came?

The restaurant was downstairs, and the steps slightly uneven as they made their way down.

The tables in the cellar were cramped. Not close enough to be touching the people at the next table, but close enough to hear their conversation. Skye darted her way through, holding some of their bags high above their heads in an attempt not to bump any elbows. They ended up at a table in the back corner, away from the main traffic.

As soon as they sat down, the waiter filled their glasses with red wine and left a single piece of paper on the table. The menu only had two choices for each course.

'What kind of place is this?' whispered Jay as he shrugged off his coat.

'A drink-what-they-give-you and eat-what-they-bring-you kind of place.' She smiled. 'It's all Scottish produce, so I've always just told them to bring what they think. I've never been disappointed.'

Jay almost held his breath at those last few words. *Never been disappointed.*

It was like there had been a low-lying hum in the air all day between them. He liked it. He liked it more than he wanted to, and more than he should.

He looked around the cellar restaurant. The ambience was good, the lighting not quite dim, but low enough to be intimate.

Most people were talking in low voices, leaning in to each other. The waiters moved seamlessly, and their wine glasses were always topped up. Jay went with the flow, and told the waiter to being whatever he recommended.

They had a lamb starter, followed by sea bass, then an intricate dessert—neither of them could work out what it was. But the array of sweet and tangy kept their tastebuds interested.

As the night continued, Jay held up his glass to admire it.

'What?' she asked.

'I've never been a red-wine fan,' he admitted.

'And now?' she asked.

'Now…' he nodded slowly '… I'm contemplating a change.'

As he sat the glass down, they looked at each other. There was so much he could say—so much they had already revealed to each other.

'I'm contemplating a change too,' she said in a hushed voice.

They both breathed quietly.

'The one thing I was sure about when I came here,' he said, 'was that I wouldn't be dating any colleague. I wanted to focus on my work.'

Skye gave a nod. 'Men have always got bored with me. I spend too much time at work, and then talk about it as soon as I get home. I always have the next day to look forward to. And, whilst I like the idea of another human in my life, I just can't prioritise it.'

'Can people really change?' he asked her, his voice husky.

'I think we can change if we want to find something else in life,' she said slowly. 'But…'

'But?' His heart was clenching in his chest. Was this where it all went wrong?

'You've barely been here a month. I don't like to jump into things.'

'You want to take things slow?'

She bit her lip. 'I think that twice we've just jumped ahead of where we should have been.'

He smiled. He couldn't help it. 'Those memories are the ones that keep me awake at night,' he admitted.

She sipped at her wine. 'They might have kept me awake too,' she conceded.

'Then what are we going to do about it?'

Skye looked thoughtful for a minute.

'We date.' She gave him a careful stare. 'And we decide if we want anyone to know about it.'

Jay shifted in his chair. He knew what she was doing. She was giving him a get-out-of-jail-free card. She knew about his past experience, and knew he didn't want their every move watched. And if they announced they were dating? The hospital grapevine would sing, and every glance, every smile and every scowl would be recorded. Every conversation with a member of the opposite sex could potentially start rumours. It was ridiculous. They both knew that.

But the reality was...had people already noticed the way he looked at her? The interactions between them? The gentle flirting? Did he really want to stop any of that?

He wasn't sure. He held up his glass. The truth was he just wanted to spend more time with her. He'd loved every moment of today, and wanted more days just like this.

'To what comes next,' he said with a smile.

'To what comes next,' agreed Skye, clinking her glass against his.

CHAPTER EIGHT

SKYE WATCHED THE man in his early fifties, who had a mild look of panic on his face.

'Can you say that again, please?' he asked.

She did. 'Mr Lucas, your cancer is at an early stage. The bowel screening test is an early indicator. The colonoscopy and biopsies have confirmed a few Stage Two areas in your bowel. A further scan shows that it doesn't look like there are any further spots. So, we'll start your treatment tomorrow if you like.'

He took his wife's hand. 'But we have a holiday planned.'

Skye gave a nod. This frequently came up with patients newly diagnosed. 'When is your holiday booked?'

'Over Christmas,' his wife said, 'but we can cancel.'

Skye took a breath. 'It's entirely up to you what you want to do. We can delay your treatment until you come back if that's what you want. But I would have to advise that you let your travel insurance company know about your diagnosis.'

'What would you do?' his wife asked.

It was the million-dollar question. Chemotherapy could make patients very ill. Should they go and have a nice holiday first? Maybe. But if they did, was there a chance the cancer could continue to develop and spread? Maybe.

Skye was always honest with her patients. She put her hand on her heart. 'I would start treatment,' she said, her mind always going to back to her father. If his cancer had been diagnosed sooner, he might have responded better to treatment. She didn't know that for sure, nobody knew that. But the little spark was still there.

'But this is your decision,' she continued. 'Why don't you go home and speak to your family and friends? I have another doctor on duty—Dr Bannerman. Do you want to speak to him as a second opinion?'

They exchanged nervous glances. 'You don't mind?'

She stood up and gave them a smile. 'Not at all. I'll go and get him.'

It only took a few moments to find Jay. The last few days with him had felt strangely like floating on some kind of cloud. The world was tinged with pink.

They'd gone to the cinema—indoors this time—and to see a pantomime in the nearby theatre. They'd also spent a few late nights working at the hospital, concentrating on the research project.

There had been no big announcement. But Skye was pretty sure that several of their colleagues were on to them. Luckily, in the run up to Christmas, people were distracted. Everyone had shopping to do, things to organise, Christmas outfits to buy and food to plan. It was a good time of year to be dating almost under the radar, and she was enjoying it.

She walked into Jay's room.

'Hey,' she said, in a tone that seemed to have been made just for him.

'Hey.' He looked up, smiling, speaking in a similar tone.

She gave a sigh and carried the tablet over. 'The fifty-two-year-old man I mentioned this morning. He's here with his wife, and they're wondering if they should go on holiday before he starts his treatment. I offered them a second opinion.'

Jay nodded, and looked over the history, the biopsy results and plan for treatment.

'No problem,' he said as he stood up.

'You're not going to ask me what I advised?' she said, a little curious.

'No,' he said, brushing the briefest kiss on her cheek. 'Because your decision will have been sound. And I don't want it to influence mine.'

He disappeared down the corridor and into her office, whilst she went to check on some other patients.

He came back a while later, his arm clearly against hers. 'He's going to start treatment tomorrow. His wife will rebook their holiday in six months when his treatment is finished, and it will coincide with their silver wedding anniversary.'

She gave him a grateful smile. He'd agreed with her opinion, and a warm feeling spread through her. She hadn't been entirely sure what he might say, because she, too, could have easily gone the other way. There could be valid arguments for both decisions. But somehow knowing he agreed with her gave her reassurance.

'Time for coffee?' he asked, and she nodded and leaned over the desk towards Indira and Ronnie.

'Can I get you guys anything from the canteen? How about the Christmas cinnamon scones?'

Ronnie patted his stomach. 'Oh, go on then, they're great.'

She gave a smile and they headed down, buying coffees for themselves and scones for the staff upstairs.

They sat down at a nearby table, and Skye couldn't help but let out a big sigh.

A furrow creased Jay's brow. 'What's up?'

She shook her head. 'Nothing really. I've just got something coming up soon that makes me nervous.'

She could tell he was surprised. 'You? But you're never nervous.'

'Of course I am,' she said quickly.

'When?' he challenged. 'On the meetings with the other research experts you are calm, confident and able to answer any question they throw at you. You give good alternatives when issues arise, and always manage to keep things on track. When hurdles come up, you problem-solve. I've never seen you nervous at all.'

She waved her hand. 'But that's entirely different. A meeting is just a few people in a room, or on the other end of a computer.'

'But you're the same with patients, their families and if you're teaching students.'

'But that's always personal too. We have a maximum of six students to teach. And they are always keen and willing to learn. This…is different.'

He leaned his head on one hand, looking a bit bemused by all this. 'Okay then, tell me what it is that's got super-researcher and doctor Skye Campbell shaking in her boots.'

'You're mocking me,' she said as she stirred her coffee. Her stomach was actually fluttering.

He slid his hand across the table and touched his fingers to hers. 'Tell me.' This time his voice was reassuring.

'So, you haven't been here at Christmas before.'

He shook his head. 'No.'

'Well, what you haven't found out yet, is that every year at Christmas there is a huge Christmas gala in aid of cancer research at the poshest hotel in Edinburgh. It's on the twenty-third of December, and…' she licked her lips, because her throat had actually just dried up '… I've been asked to speak at it.'

'But that's fantastic. You're the perfect person to speak at it. I can't think of anyone more qualified.'

She put her hand to her throat, now feeling a bit sick. She swallowed. 'But that's just the thing. I hate public speaking. I get nervous in crowds. I just look out and see a sea of faces.' She intertwined her fingers with his and squeezed. Maybe a little bit too hard.

He crooked his head. 'But haven't you had to do it for things before?'

She took a breath and closed her eyes. 'Well, I had to do some presentations at university during medical training. But they broke us into groups. So, it wasn't the whole class of a hundred and twenty.' She shuddered. 'It was a maximum of fifteen people in the class. That I could just about manage.'

'Have you ever spoken in front of a crowd? Maybe it's just because you haven't done it before.'

She pulled a face. 'Well, I've not. But I've won a few awards, and any time my name was called, I swear, my heart was racing, my hands were sweating and I felt as if I couldn't breathe. I couldn't even say thank you in a normal voice, let alone do a thank you speech.' She tugged at her shirt. 'I'm feeling nervous just thinking about it.'

Jay looked thoughtful. 'Why? What is it that just makes you so nervous?'

She pulled her fingers back from his, and started drumming them on the table. It was hard to put things into words. She'd never really talked to anyone about this before.

She looked up—his brown eyes were fixed on hers. 'It's personal,' she said. 'I would be okay if it was about the research, or cancer signs and symptoms, and treatments. I could talk about all that until the cows come home.' She stopped for a breath. 'But they asked me to talk about my experience. About how my dad getting cancer and dying changed my course in life, and how I'm now devoted to this.'

'And that's great.' She could see him thinking. 'You managed to tell me about it.'

She held up her hands. 'But that was different. It was just you and me. It wasn't a room filled with four hundred people expecting me to talk from the heart about something that still impacts me.'

Jay stayed silent for so long that she wondered if he was just going to give up on her.

When he spoke, he kept his voice low. 'Grief has no timespan. It's one of the biggest lessons I've learned when treating patients with cancer. People always assume that in a few years they'll feel better after losing a relative. And for some people, in a couple of years, they can start to get their life back. But, one of the first doctors I worked with had lost a child. And it didn't get better. Every birthday was a memory lost. Milestones that his child would never reach.

He was haunted by it. And who had the right to tell him he shouldn't feel grief?' He reached over and took her hand again. 'It's the same for your father.' He kept his voice low again. 'You would have wanted him to see you graduate as a doctor?'

Her skin prickled and she sniffed, feeling tears well up in her eyes. She just gave a nod.

'You would have wanted your dad to walk you down the aisle at some point, and hopefully one day hold your first baby?' The tears started to fall. He wasn't saying any of this to be mean, and she knew that. He was telling her that he understood. She nodded again.

Jay reached over and caught one of her tears with his thumb. 'I don't want you to be unhappy. If this is making you feel like this, should you be doing it?'

She hated herself right now. Hated herself for crying in the hospital canteen—she could see glances being cast their way. The very thing that Jay had not wanted. But to be fair, he didn't look as if he was noticing.

'Do you think I should back out?' Her voice was breaking.

'I think you should do what you feel is right,' he said in a smooth tone. 'They asked you to do this because they want to hear your story. But it's entirely up to you if you want to share. No one can force you to do it.'

'What good would it do?'

Jay looked at her carefully and licked his lips, clearly considering what to say. His gaze was sincere. 'I think you could do a lot of good. I think you might give hope to some people, fire to others and comfort to some. Remember that most people who support cancer research or cancer charities have been affected in some way. It could be that some are struggling with grief. Maybe they too could channel how they feel another way? Maybe they just need to hear that, even though it's been a few years, you still have full, vibrant memories of your dad. Some people are scared they might forget things. You're going to prove to them that you don't.'

The tears were still falling, but his words were a big comfort. He was making sense. She hadn't really considered this point of view before.

Jay kept going. 'You might inspire other people to be doctors, nurses or researchers. To volunteer. To raise money for the research.'

Skye nodded—she was feeling calmer. He was helping. He was giving her a bit of confidence to know that her talking might be important and might inspire others.

'Do you have a date?' he asked.

The question caught her unawares and she let out a laugh. 'What?'

'A date. Is someone going with you?'

She shook her head. 'No. I hadn't even planned ahead. I still wasn't sure I could actually do it.'

'How about I come with you—only if you want, of course.'

She smiled at him. This guy, who'd started here prickly and pushing everyone away. The same guy who didn't really want people in the hospital talking about him, but hadn't been afraid to reach out and take her hand in the middle of the canteen.

'I'll give you a pep talk on the way there. I'll distract you, keep your mind off things. Anything you want really.'

She said the only thing her heart would let her. 'You don't need to sell yourself. I'd love it if you came with me.'

CHAPTER NINE

IF HE WAS HONEST, Jay was feeling a tiny bit nervous himself. He'd checked his bowtie at least five times before he'd climbed in the car to pick up Skye.

He'd asked her about her dress but she'd been very coy, just saying it was something special.

As he rang the door, he wondered if the flowers he'd brought was going overboard. But the expression on her face as she opened the door told him everything he needed to know.

'Oh, they're beautiful,' she said, taking the large bouquet of Christmas flowers from his hands. Red, greens, whites and golds along with a huge red bow in an already filled clear glass vase, meaning Skye could carry them straight to her table in the hall.

As she turned, he caught a glimpse of green sequin. Once she sat the flowers down and spun around, he got the full effect.

'Wow,' was all he could say.

She grinned. 'You like?' She gestured with her hands to the full-length green sequined dress that hugged her body perfectly. The top had a low V and thick straps. Her dark curls were styled around her shoulders, her green eyes looking darker than normal alongside her pale skin and red lips.

'You look stunning,' he breathed, wondering how on earth he got so lucky. 'How are you feeling?' he asked, remembering his role here today.

He stepped inside and put his hand on her hips. She gestured back to the table where she'd sat the flowers. Now he noticed the shredded paper. 'What's going on?'

She picked up a silver sequin bag and held it up.

'It's tiny,' he said, stating the obvious.

She nodded. 'Room for my house key, my phone and lipstick. That's it.'

Jay glanced at the paper. He could swear that at some point there had been writing on it. 'So, what is that—your speech?'

She nodded. But she didn't look worried. Her spine was straight, her shoulders back. 'I decided I didn't need it. I'd written it five times, scored parts out, and it was actually making me worse.'

He noticed the tiny tremor in her hands and took them both, pressing them up to his chest.

'Speak from the heart, that's all that matters and all that counts.'

She nodded her head and took a deep breath. 'You're right. Now let's go.'

He put her black coat around her shoulders and they headed outside.

By the time they reached the hotel, there was a queue of cars. He squeezed her hand. 'Well, at least you don't need to worry about the biggest disaster for a fundraiser event.'

'What do you mean?'

He smiled. 'No one turning up. Look at the queue, that's fantastic.'

She gave a tiny groan. 'Think of the all the people in the room.'

'No. Don't. Only think of the people in the room when there's a fundraising moment and they do one of those charity auctions.'

She nodded her head, as if she were trying to convince herself. The car edged forward again until they were finally in front of the hotel. Because it was one of the main roads in Edinburgh, valet parking was a must. So when the suited valet appeared with a ticket in his hand, Jay jumped out to take it, before coming around to take Skye's hand as she emerged from the car.

There was a tiny second—as the ripples of her dress fell into place around her body—when he caught his breath. Did she have any idea how beautiful she was?

They walked up the steps to the hotel and through the main doors, instantly hit with a wave of heat.

It only took a few seconds to see how seriously this hotel took Christmas. The tree in the main entrance was huge, and it looked real, decorated in silver. The pink and purple logo of the cancer charity was matched by subtle decorations throughout the room.

It was only a few moments before they were offered a drink from a silver tray and ushered through to the ballroom.

Skye stopped mid-step, and he instantly understood why. The ballroom was spectacular, with a stage at one end, the silver, pink and purple theme carried on throughout, with around one hundred and fifty tables set, filling out the room. The bar at one side was the whole length of the ballroom and already had wait staff dashing back and forward from it, carrying trays.

Whilst he thought the place was spectacular, he could see it entirely from Skye's point of view. Volume.

He heard her shaky breath as he slipped his arm around her waist. 'Just be you. They will love you.' He kissed her cheek and she gave a nod of her head.

She slid her hand into his and they made their way across the ballroom, greeting the hosts and sitting at one of the tables near the front. It wasn't just Skye who was talking tonight. There was a whole host of entertainment for the gala, as well as a charity raffle, followed by a full-on disco.

The room filled quickly as people in spectacular outfits found their tables. The hotel kept things running smoothly, ensuring hors d'oeuvres and drinks flowed. It would have been easy to take another glass of the bubbles, but Jay had seen that Skye was sticking to her original glass and had only taken a few small sips. So, he decided to do the same.

There was a room reserved at the hotel in their name, so Jay didn't need to worry about driving later.

He could see her taking deep breaths and forcing herself to relax. He gently sat his hand on her leg underneath the table, and she dropped her own hand on top of his, squeezing it in appreciation.

'Ready?' he asked quietly. As he leaned in, he could smell her perfume again, and for a moment he wondered how he'd ended up here.

Here. With Skye. Feeling like this.

The compere for the gala started, and a few entertainers came on, getting the spirits in the room high. Both he and Skye laughed at the comedian, and watched in awe at the magician, trying to work out how he did his tricks. Then, one of the charity choirs came on to sing a host of Christmas tunes. Food appeared before them as if by magic, with the plates swept away as soon as they were finished. The hotel staff had this all down to a fine art.

Then, the chairperson of the cancer research committee appeared to remind everyone why they were here, and why their work was so vitally important in the fight against cancer.

This was it. This was Skye's moment. As her name was called, he saw her momentarily freeze. Her whole body went rigid, her face like stone.

He moved his arm back around her waist and whispered in her ear. 'You are a wonderful doctor, and a great daughter. Go and tell the people how much you love your dad, and how your work honours his memory.'

She gave the briefest shiver, as if something had just danced along the length of her spine, then she turned to him, her face relaxed but with a determined air. 'You bet I will.'

As she climbed the stairs to the stage, and

stood behind the podium, Jay had only one thought. He'd never loved this woman more.

Skye had been momentarily stunned with nerves, but having Jay by her side, being her cheerleader, was exactly what she'd needed. Before she'd spoken to him, she'd started to build this thing up in her head to something unachievable.

But now she was here. All five versions of the speech she'd tried to write had shot from her mind like a cannon ball, leaving no trace behind. But as she looked around the sea of faces, a few started to stand out. A patient she'd treated. Another who'd recently had a baby. Colleagues who worked in other areas. All pieces of a jig-saw puzzle that made up parts of her life.

Then there was Jay. The guy who'd appeared out of nowhere like the baddie in a Christmas movie, who finds the joy of Christmas, and turns his life around.

But it was her life that was turning around from the impact they were having on each other. She was finding it hard to admit to herself how much she was falling for him.

She didn't want to. She didn't want to end up disappointed. Wouldn't he eventually go back to London? She knew her old supervisor's knee replacement had gone well and he was currently in rehab. But once he was back to full health, he would be expected to return on a permanent basis. So where would that leave Jay?

They hadn't even talked about that. But then again, they hadn't really talked about *them* either. Was there even a them?

As she stood on the podium under the spotlight, a wave of emotions flooded through her. As she blinked under the bright lights, her eyes went to one place. Jay.

As handsome as any film star, sitting in his tuxedo and bowtie, as if he were waiting for the Oscar ceremony to start. His slightly tousled hair, the shadow along his strong jaw line, and— if she had been close enough to see them—those brown eyes that would be cheering her on. She knew that.

She'd never felt like this about anyone before. She'd never been so drawn to someone, or at times so annoyed by them. His accent made her want to float. His touch made her want to cry. His kisses took her to a whole other place.

In general, he made her want to sing, like one of those cartoon princesses with an array of animals forming a choir. If only they would do her housework too.

'Skye?'

A voice made her jolt, and she realised the chairperson was looking at her with concern.

She breathed, smiled, pushed her shoulders back and adjusted the microphone.

'Thank you for joining us tonight at this Christmas gala in aid of cancer research. My name is Dr Skye Campbell, and I have both professional and personal reasons for being here. Let me tell you why.'

Her stomach was doing its own version of a ceilidh. But she wanted to do justice to the invite she'd been given. So, she started by telling stories about her dad. The fun relationship they'd had. The time she'd slipped over in the waves at the beach, and her father had practically stampeded over everyone to get to her. The time she'd refused to attend ballet because she wanted to do karate, and he'd marched her across the road in her tutu, immediately putting her in the other class.

How proud he'd been when she'd been accepted into medicine. How sad they'd both been when she'd moved from home to the university halls to begin her new life.

How excited she'd been at first, then how she'd noticed a change in her dad when she'd visited for holidays. The small and seemingly unimportant symptoms, which had never been alarming but merely annoying. The way that neither she, nor her parents, had put things together until it reached a crisis point.

How she'd been devastated by his diagnosis, and the progression of the disease. How it had made her channel all her focus at university into studying cancer. How she, and her mother, had nursed her father at the end. How unfair everything felt. How unfair it still felt. How, the what-if game still played in her mind. What if she'd stayed at home and made her father take his mild symptoms more seriously? What if he'd visited the doctor sooner, and started treatment much earlier? What if doing those things would've meant he'd still be here today?

How even now, years on, those thoughts still haunted her. Skye knew that her voice was cracking. She knew she was shedding tears on the stage. But the only thing she was aware of was the fact that she could practically hear a pin drop.

She told them how she'd focused on becoming a doctor of research, as well as a doctor of medicine. She talked about the importance of research to give a better understanding of the disease, and how to stop it. She talked about AI, and embracing technology that might give them the answers they needed. She joked about *Star Trek*, and the fact she was sure that one day they would indeed have a medical tricorder, which could tell them what's happening in the human body in an instant.

She talked about some forms of cancer—like high-risk neuroblastoma in children, where five-year survival rates were still not great.

She put her hand on her heart, and told them that she honestly believed that someday, in the future, they would find a cure for cancer, and that she dearly believed it would be in her lifetime. And that every time they supported a cancer research charity, they were helping to do that.

By the time she was finished, Skye felt exhausted. At first there was silence, then applause erupted around the room, and the whole room stood on their feet.

The chairperson came to her side sniffing, and thanking her, saying there wasn't a dry eye in the house, and she managed to grab her dress and get down those steps to her table again.

Jay wrapped his arms around her, and she let herself just fall into them. It was so nice to have someone here. Someone who believed in her and supported her. Who knew her history, and why she did this. Someone who'd told her she could do this.

'I'm so proud,' he whispered in her ear. 'You were magnificent.' He released from their cuddle and held her by the shoulders, looking into her eyes. 'And I just know that your dad would be so proud of you, too.'

He wiped her tears and handed her a drink. She looked at it blankly for a moment. 'You told me your favourite cocktail the other day. I ordered it in advance.'

As she took a sip, she was surrounded by well-wishers, all thanking her for her speech and telling her how it affected them. It was as if her speech had caused a buzz across the room, and as the next part of the evening was the charity auction, it seemed it couldn't have been better timed.

For the next hour, she relaxed into Jay, sipping her cocktail and watching the auction. A whole host of weird and wonderful items were bid on in the room, as well as online. Some of the amounts were staggering, and word was that some celebrities had decided to bid online in support.

By the time the auction was finished, the total amount raised was flashed up on a screen over the stage, and it made her cry again.

An array of canapes were set up in the adjoining room, and guests were encouraged to move through whilst the dance floor and the band were set up.

As they moved through the crowds, hand in

hand, people were still stopping to speak to her, to tell their stories and offer their support.

After a while, Jay gave her a nudge and whispered in a low voice. 'Fancy some air?'

She nodded gratefully and the two of them stepped outside into the cold Edinburgh night. He slipped his jacket around her shoulders. 'Okay?'

She nodded and smiled. Her heart was happy— it felt as if she'd done a good thing tonight. 'I just feel exhausted,' she admitted. 'I'm not sure how long I can last on the dancefloor.'

'Then why don't we have a party of our own?'

She gave him a secret smile. 'What do you mean?'

'I mean, I booked us a room here. Just in case it all got too much for you. I wanted you to have somewhere you could go if you needed some time out.'

'You did?' She was surprised and more than a little flattered by his consideration. Then she frowned. 'I heard the rooms were booked out months ago.'

He smiled. 'They probably were, and we just got lucky when I phoned.' He pulled a key from his pocket. 'Want to go and see?'

She leaned forward, putting her hands on his chest, noticing instantly how cold his shirt was already. 'Some women might be suspicious of this planning,' she teased. 'They might think you were trying to send them a message.'

His breath was warm on her face. 'We've been sending each other messages for weeks. Honestly, I didn't tell you about the room because I didn't want you to think that. If I was a better planner, I would have warned you in advance to bring some overnight clothes—likely some fleecy pyjamas.' He gave a wicked smile as he held up his hands. 'But it seems I forgot.'

He licked his lips and looked down at her through his thick lashes. 'I still only had a few sips. If you want to go home I can collect my car, I can take you home right now.'

She looked thoughtful for a moment, though she'd made up her mind instantly. 'I have a better idea. How about we slope off to the bar for an hour and get a bit tipsy? Then we can head up the stairs.'

'Your wish is my command,' he said as he put his arm back around her, leading her up the steps and into the dark wood-panelled bar. They sat in deep comfortable leather armchairs whilst their waiter brought them a bottle of champagne.

'If you'd told me five weeks ago this is where I'd be, and this is who I'd be with, I might not have believed you.' She smiled as they clinked their glasses.

'What's that supposed to mean?' he said, but he had a big grin on his face. He put one hand on his chest. 'You say that as if my reputation had preceded me.'

She leaned forward, giving him a clear, intentional view of her cleavage. 'I have no idea what you mean,' she replied, letting his eyes linger before she sat back up.

Her mind was swirling. Maybe it was the champagne. Maybe it was just how overwhelming the night had been. But all of a sudden, she was considering what it might be like to have it all.

To be able to come home to someone at night. To have a loving relationship and successful career, in a way she'd never thought possible before.

Little voices played in the back of her head. Jay wasn't here permanently. She knew that. He would have to leave, and likely soon. But, for five minutes, couldn't she pretend to have it all? Her heart was bursting tonight. She'd spent so long living in fear.

Once you'd lost someone you loved to cancer, a permanent guard formed around you. Going through the pain once was bad enough—the thought of loving someone again, and risking losing them, was just too much.

But right now, it was just her and Jay, and the most wonderful time of year. 'Would it be terrible if I told you I wanted one dance before we go upstairs?'

He gave her a guarded look. 'And what might that dance be to?'

'Just my favourite Christmas song of all time.'

He groaned and leaned forward. 'I'm going to have to do a request, aren't I?'

She smiled broadly. 'I'm sure it's on their playlist. Will you ask for "Last Christmas"?'

He sat down his champagne glass as he narrowed his gaze a little. 'Isn't that a sad song?'

'Not when you're dancing with your perfect person,' she replied.

Jay disappeared out of his chair, and within a few moments he was back. He held out his hand to her. 'You're in luck, or you just have perfect timing. We're up.'

She slid her hand into his and they made their way back into the ballroom. The Christmas lights were twinkling, the main lights dimmed and she let Jay lead her to the middle of the floor as the first notes started.

They'd never danced together before, but Jay had rhythm and Jay had moves. Even though she was pressed up close to him, and could feel the heat from his body next to hers, he spun her around the dance floor as if they'd been dancing partners for years. It was a slow song, but by the time they were finished she was giddy, laughing as she kept her arms wrapped around his neck and his mouth firmly on hers.

'Take me upstairs,' she murmured as she ran her fingers down the length of his spine.

His dark eyes fixed on hers. 'Are you sure?'

'I've never been surer,' she replied, meaning it from the top of her forehead to the tips of her toes. Nothing had ever been as magical as tonight.

CHAPTER TEN

JAY WOKE UP in the pristine linen sheets—the feel of Skye's body next to his—and couldn't be happier.

Things had changed rapidly between them. It had been inevitable—they both knew that. And from the moment they'd entered the room last night, they hadn't wasted any time. He smiled at the clothes lying littered around the room and wondered if they might find them all this morning.

He couldn't remember ever feeling like this. Not even with Jessica. It was only hindsight that meant he could see it.

Should he order breakfast? Neither of them were officially scheduled to work today. It might be nice to have some room service before they decided what they would do with the rest of the day.

He stroked one finger down the side of Skye's face. She was lying with her back to him and breathing slowly.

'Hey,' he murmured, 'happy Christmas Eve.'

There was a moan, and then a murmur, before she turned around to face him.

He didn't wait for her to open her eyes. 'I've been thinking,' he said. 'That this connection between us,' his fingers were still touching her skin, this time her shoulder, 'is so strong, we shouldn't ignore it. We should listen. We should see where this takes us. Embrace it.'

Her eyes opened. She still looked sleepy. And she hadn't spoken, so he just continued.

'I know I'm heading back to London soon, and I've never had a long-distance relationship before. But I think we should try—if you want to. I don't want to walk away from this. This… This isn't casual.' His fingers moved from her shoulder, and he very gently traced one down her cheek. 'Not for me, anyhow.'

She blinked, and he wasn't sure what it was he could see behind her eyes. But she surprised him with her sudden movement—she sat up suddenly and leaned back against the pillows.

'I think we should keep seeing each other,' he pressed. 'I think we should see where this goes.'

Skye was terrified. Terrified by everything.

By the strength of her feelings last night, the

connection between them and, most of all, by the way her heart was telling her to hold on tight.

And that onslaught of emotions was sending her into panic mode. Jay was right here. Right beside her. On one hand telling her that he was leaving, but on the other that he wanted to make this work.

She felt as if she couldn't breathe. Everything had been so perfect. Like the final scene in a film. And everyone knew that all the characters got their happily ever after following the final scene. So what was wrong with her?

She blinked her eyes and knew in an instant. When you loved someone this hard, what happened if you lost them?

A car crash, a bad flight, an electric storm, a disease. A rogue cell growing into something it shouldn't.

A look or a glance from someone else once Jay got back down to London. A beautiful, intelligent woman, who wasn't emotionally stunted like she was, who would feel free to love and embrace him. He might feel this connection again, and it wouldn't be with her. What then? A broken heart that she might never recover from?

It was truly amazing what could flash through the human brain in the blink of an eye.

She'd been through the heartbreak of losing someone before. And whilst she knew that a family member was different to a romantic partner, at the end of the day, it came down to a similar premise. Love.

She'd learned how to be resilient. She'd had to. And maybe that was part of why no relationship had really worked for her—she hadn't put herself out there. She'd been too scared. Too cautious. Letting herself love someone else would instantly put her heart at risk. Could she actually cope with that?

And what about Jay? The guy with the deep brown eyes that sent her spiralling, the gorgeous accent, the gentle touch that was like an electricity bolt to all her senses.

She wanted it. She wanted it all. She wanted him. But the truth was—she was just too scared.

His eyes were fixed on hers. Her chest was tight. But she needed to talk. She needed to give him an answer—even if she knew it wasn't what he wanted to hear.

'I'm not sure,' she finally said.

Jay flinched, almost as if she'd slapped him with the palm of her hand. His face had had a dreamy quality about it only seconds before, and it was clear that he'd thought she would agree with what he said.

'We've never talked about long-term,' she

said quickly, wishing for all the world that she wasn't actually naked under these sheets with an equally naked Jay next to her. 'Long-term has never been in the picture. You came up here for six weeks to supervise the research project. A project that I still need to work on.'

Her voice became a little more impassioned. 'You've seen me. You've seen how many hours a day it takes up, over and above the day job. How on earth do you think it's even feasible to carry on a long-term relationship when I have those kind of work hours? It's not realistic, no matter what way you try to stretch it.'

Her heart was clenched in her chest right now, because Jay's face told her everything she needed to know. He was devastated, and it was her who'd done this to him.

She honestly didn't deserve him.

She swallowed and tugged at the sheet on the bed, keeping it against her chest as she stood up and looked frantically around the room for her clothes. What had happened to her bra?

She caught a flash of sequin and made a grab for her dress, hauling it up her body in a way it probably wasn't designed to go.

Jay sat upright. His face was pure confusion. 'This is honestly how you want things to go?'

She took a shaky breath as her dress finally

adjusted into place and she located her shoes. She dropped the sheet.

'It has to.' She struggled to navigate her feet into their strappy shoes. 'This could never work for us. Not really. I have to focus on the project. I can't get distracted. I have to put all my time and energy into the thing that could make a difference to people. You heard me talk last night. You know where my heart lies.'

She couldn't look at him. Not now. She couldn't look into those brown eyes knowing what she'd just done.

It was true. What she'd said was entirely true. She should focus everything on the research project. It was the best thing to do for herself, and to pay tribute to her dad.

She picked up her black coat and swallowed, her throat horribly dry. She couldn't look at him as she left.

'You're a wonderful person, Jay. I'm sure you'll find the right person soon.'

And with those final words, she walked out the door before she started to cry.

Jay was numb. He couldn't believe what had just happened.

More than that, he couldn't believe he'd been such a fool.

He'd been burned once, he should have learned his lesson then. But no, he had to be a fool and misread a situation totally.

He put his head in his hands. It didn't seem real. He'd finally found someone he'd felt a real connection with. Someone he thought he could trust.

He'd thought Skye Campbell was worth the risk. Worth the risk of opening up his heart again and taking a chance on love.

But he'd been wrong. So wrong that he kept rethinking things in his head.

The dates, the flirting, the buzz between them. Their first kiss, and then their second. All of last night and just how magical it had been for him—for them—or so he'd thought. Had he been living in fairy land? Had all this just been a game to Skye?

He'd been sorry. Sorry at the thought of having to leave Edinburgh and go back to London. He'd already been half thinking about trying to find another job in Scotland. Thank goodness he hadn't taken any steps.

He pulled out his phone, searching for the first flight down to London. He didn't even care which airport. He would worry about his father's car later. The lease on the house had been twelve weeks minimum, so he could still leave the car there until he got things sorted.

But in the meantime, all he wanted to do was get away. He didn't even care about his clothes and other items he'd left at the house. He looked at his jacket hanging over the back of the chair. He could hardly fly home in a tux—he supposed he could collect the minimum of his personal belongings. What did he even actually need?

As he walked about the room searching for his clothes, he was cursing himself the whole way.

He'd fallen hard. He should never have let himself. From the moment she'd sparked his attention he should have just shut down and kept himself and his heart safe.

This wasn't worth it. And even worse, it was Christmas. He didn't have any plans. His sister was already off to his parents' house and he would never turn up unexpectedly. That would only result in a whole host of questions he just didn't want to answer.

But even he knew it was the worst time of year to be alone. Christmas seemed to echo louder amongst those who were alone, and he wasn't prepared for that. His penthouse flat back in London would be pristine. That is to say, bland and undecorated. He didn't have a single piece of food in the fridge and likely only a few random things in the freezer. He wasn't even sure he'd have enough time to food shop after he landed. His Christmas food might end up being whatever was on sale at the airport and his packet of emergency digestive biscuits. Fantastic. Happy Christmas.

As he fastened his shirt and picked up his wallet he groaned. People would have seen them last night. Lots of people, and likely word would have spread quickly.

It almost felt as if the Great Southern and Great Northern had some kind of grapevine all of its own. If he had thought things were bad before at the Southern, he would be lucky if he was only known as a laughing stock now.

But something struck him.

Did he really care? Did he really care what other people thought of him and his disaster of a love life?

He grabbed his jacket and keys. *No.* No, he didn't. And what did it matter anyway? Because there was no love life to speak of. And that's exactly the way it would continue.

CHAPTER ELEVEN

SKYE WAS MOVING on autopilot. She stumbled out the hotel—ignoring the stares of other guests in reception, as it looked as though she was doing the walk of shame from the night before—grabbed a taxi and sobbed all the way home.

It was Christmas Eve, and she wasn't scheduled to work. But work was always Skye's solace. So, she scrubbed her face, tugged on some thick woolly tights and the first piece of clothing she came across, and headed straight back to the Great Northern.

If people were surprised to see her, they didn't say so. She'd grabbed a coffee and muffin on the way in, and after a quick check to make sure all the patients were fine, she headed into her office, closing the door behind her with a sigh—and then another sob.

As she looked at the piles and piles of medical records in front of her, a new sensation swamped her. Was this it? Was this it for her life?

And was this it because she'd chosen it?

Her phone beeped and she looked down at the text.

Catching a flight to London. Will continue to support the project.

Her heart stopped. That was it. Nothing else. But what did she expect?

She'd seen Jay only a few hours ago, but she was missing him already. The realisation hit her like a snowball to the head.

She picked up the coat she'd just taken off and brought it to her nose. There it was. An indistinguishable scent to others, but distinctive to her. She could smell the faint aroma of his aftershave. She'd been with him the last time she'd worn this coat.

As she breathed in, she had a startling realisation. She loved him. She loved Jay Bannerman. She loved his tousled brown hair, his deep dark eyes, the little lines around his eyes, and that fantastic voice. She loved the way he frowned, and how he had just as much of a work ethic as she did. She loved the way he'd embraced his sense of fun, when he'd started at the Northern so buttoned up. She loved the way he'd admitted to his own apparent weak points—that he hated being talked about—and that made her stomach plummet. He'd trusted her with that information, and what had she done?

She started to feel sick now. The aroma of sweetness from the muffin and coffee weren't helping. She'd done everything wrong.

A man she adored had proposed a way forward for them both. And instead of grabbing it with both hands, and shouting her glee from the rooftops, she'd disappeared quicker than a rat down a drainpipe.

A rat. It felt like an apt description right now.

She took a deep breath and tried to be rational. She could remember all those fleeting thoughts in the hotel room that had filled her heart with fear. The risk of loving someone else. The risk of losing someone else, and wondering if she could ever survive it.

Her stomach clenched. Those feelings were still there.

There was a knock at the door and Indira stuck her head in. 'If you wouldn't mind, could you have a quick check over Mr Lucas's medications? He's feeling really queasy and needs something to settle his stomach.' Her brow creased. 'You look terrible, by the way. Anything I should know?'

Indira. Always a defender of the truth. Just

what she didn't need. 'No, everything's fine. I'll be there in a minute.' Indira nodded and left.

She sighed and put her head on the desk for a moment, taking a few breaths. Mr Lucas, the man who should currently be on holiday, but who'd agreed to stay and start treatment. Most of the patients should be getting day passes for Christmas Day to go home and spend time with their families. She would need to make sure he was fit enough to do that.

She left the office and picked up her tablet to check his meds before she got to him. He'd been moved into one of the side rooms and, as she approached, she could hear people talking.

It was Mr Lucas and his wife. Both sounded upset, and she stopped, not wanting to intrude on a personal moment.

Normally she would move away, not listening to what was being said, but for some reason the few words she did hear made her feet almost stick to the floor.

'But what if I don't get better? What if this treatment makes me sicker than ever?'

'Don't say that, honey. They always say you'll feel worse before you feel better. It's just a bad day.'

His voice cracked. 'The Bahamas was always your dream. I'm sorry it took us twenty-five years to book it. We should have gone sooner. We should have started our bucket list whilst we were still young and fit.'

'Don't say that. We'll still get to the Bahamas. We'll still get to all the places on our list.'

'But what if we don't?'

Skye could hear the anguish in his voice.

But his wife's voice was calm and assured. She spoke with complete and utter conviction. 'Then I have no regrets. John, I married you because I loved you, and because I wanted to spend all my time with you. It doesn't matter where in the world we are, what's important to me is that I'm with you.'

'But all those extra hours at work. All those missed weekends. All the business trips that I should have sent someone else on, but insisted I had to go myself.' He sounded tearful. 'I'm sorry. I should never have let work prioritise my life for me. I should have never thought it was more important than us, more important than you. I should have spent all that time with you. And here I am now, lying in bed, ruining your Christmas for you. You love Christmas Eve. It's your favourite time of the year. We used to make a day of it, taking the kids out for lunch and then going to see whatever blockbuster was on at the cinema. I can't even keep water down right now.' His voice dropped low. 'You probably regret dancing with me all those years ago.' He gave a choked laugh. 'You should have picked the other guy.'

The wife's voice came back, strong and solid. 'Stop it,' she said firmly. 'There's no room for regrets here. Everyone could live a better life with hindsight if they knew what was ahead, but we've not been granted that gift. I wouldn't change a thing about our life, and I don't have regrets. We met when we were supposed to meet. I wasn't supposed to dance with the other guy, I was supposed to dance with you. The time we've had is precious and it will continue to be. I fully intend to make wonderful memories for our twenty-fifth wedding anniversary in the Bahamas. We've had plenty of great Christmases. And we'll make this one our own too—even if it has to be different. What's important, and what's always important, is that we are together.'

His voice was croaky. 'I know they said they caught it early. I know they said there is a good chance of success. But what if that isn't me? What if this is terminal? I don't want you to have a miserable few years because I'm sick.'

'John Lucas. That's enough. In sickness and in health. That's the vow we made. It could just as easily be me in that bed instead of you. I know you. I know you would do exactly what I'm going to do—stay by your side. We're a team. I don't regret a single minute with you, and I'm going to celebrate every single minute I can get.'

There was a reason her feet were frozen to the floor—it flooded over her like a tidal wave. It didn't matter that she shouldn't have eavesdropped. It had struck every nerve she had. Because, despite the crushing weight of grief from losing her dad, she did not regret a single minute she'd spent with him. That had always been blindingly clear to her.

All moments were precious.

Skye almost choked. The fear that had been sitting all around her, like a hidden barrier, just needed to be stepped through. She had no guarantee of what lay ahead for her, or for Jay, but what she did know was that she didn't want to waste a single minute. She wanted to grab the chance of a relationship with him—a chance of her own happily ever after—with both hands.

For a moment, she thought she might be sick as she remembered the look on his face when she'd made excuses not to be together—not to give them both a chance.

She glanced at the ward clock, then back at the tablet in her hand. She had a duty to try and make John Lucas feel better, to try and make

Christmas pleasant for him. Once she'd finished with her patients, she would do a mad dash to the airport.

A single tear fell down her cheek. She could only hope that Jay would forgive her.

CHAPTER TWELVE

JAY HAD ALWAYS loved his London home. But right now it just felt empty.

The heating was on, he still had his gorgeous view of Canary Wharf and he'd managed to grab a few things from the posh supermarket at the station on his way back. It was hardly Christmas food, but it was better than an empty fridge.

As he padded across the floor of the living room and stared out at the view, all he could notice was the echo around him, the emptiness.

Jay Bannerman had always liked his own space. He'd loved buying his own place after house-sharing with others. He'd taken pride in decorating and the upkeep of it. He'd never noticed before that there seemed to be a few things missing.

He shook his head. He was feeling melancholy, it was just the time of year. It did this to lots of people. Maybe he should have thought about joining his parents and sister, but since he'd left his car in Scotland that would be tough. And it had just started to snow—the road to Brighton wouldn't be clear.

He sighed, wishing he had some Christmas decorations. He did have some in a box some place, but they were right at the back of a cupboard that he had no energy to rummage through.

He was trying so hard not to let his mind go back to this morning. He'd spent the whole flight going over things in his head, wondering how he'd got it all so massively wrong.

Was he just a really poor judge of women? Or was he just not capable of the type of commitment a relationship needed? Maybe that's what she'd been trying to tell him?

He contemplated a beer. He'd bought a whole four and they were in the fridge. He'd just started walking to the kitchen when there was a buzz at his door.

He frowned. He certainly wasn't expecting anyone. And to be honest, he wasn't in the mood for company.

It must be a neighbour. Anyone else would have buzzed from the main entrance. He'd never had an unexpected neighbour visit, and he hoped they didn't want to borrow the traditional sugar or milk—because he didn't have any.

He sighed as he opened the door, and his breath caught somewhere in his throat.

Skye. Looking more than a little dishevelled. Her cheeks were pink, her hair sticking out everywhere. But what surprised him most was the fact she looked just as shellshocked as he felt.

'I'm sorry,' she said rapidly. 'I'm so, so sorry. I just freaked out this morning. I panicked. Can I come in?'

He stepped back automatically, not really finding words.

She stepped inside and paused. 'Whoa.'

He closed the door. She was staring straight at the view, caught unawares by the sight of London stretched out before her.

He moved beside her, but didn't speak.

After a few seconds she turned back to face him. But then she kind of crumpled and put her face in both hands.

He could hear her breathing heavily.

'Do you want to sit down?' he asked, not entirely sure if that was wise or not.

She didn't answer for a second, then pulled her hands back. Her eyes had filled with tears. She nodded, shrugging off her black coat as she sat on his cream sofa.

Her voice was shaky. 'I behaved really badly

this morning, and I hurt you. I should never have done that.'

He just looked at her, trying to take in the fact that he'd been thinking about her five minutes before, and now she was in front of him.

'You came from Edinburgh? On Christmas Eve?'

She was starting to shake. 'I didn't know what else to do. I couldn't phone you. I couldn't text. No one who has screwed up as much as I did should apologise like that. I had to do it in person.'

Now he was starting to get annoyed. 'But this morning you were sure about things. You said what was on your mind and left.'

She shook her head. 'I said what a panicked idiot says, when the man she's fallen in love with offers her a chance of a real relationship that she doesn't think she's worthy of.'

'What?'

There was a long silence between them. She put a hand to her chest and gave him a sad smile.

'Jay Bannerman, I wonder if you've actually realised I'm a complete mess? My life is all about work. I tell myself it's because I'm devoted to it, but the truth is, and I only just got this myself, it's because I'm too scared to let myself love someone. I'm too scared to take the risk that I might lose that person.' She shook her head. 'I've suffered loss. I came out other side, and I just don't know if I can do that again.' The tears were flowing down her cheeks. 'Or I thought I couldn't. But then I heard Mr and Mrs Lucas talking today. Talking about every minute counting, no matter what.'

She shook her head again and looked at him with pleading eyes. 'I've just done all of this wrong. I didn't want to like you—I really didn't. But I couldn't help it, I just did.' She held up both hands. 'I couldn't ignore the buzz between us, I've never felt anything like that before, then that first time you kissed me...' Her voice tailed off.

It was like someone put their fist around his heart and squeezed. He felt this, he really did. But he just didn't know how to deal with it.

He couldn't live like this, catapulting from one emotion to the other. This morning he'd started the day happy, then been devastated at her words and actions. Now, hours later, she was here, taking it all back?

He held up his hand. 'I can't do this. I can't rollercoaster from one minute to the next. *I* wanted things to work this morning, and you didn't. You didn't want any kind of relationship with me, and certainly didn't want to work at it.

You can't just change your mind and turn up at my door as if that didn't happen.'

'I'm sorry,' she said. 'I didn't mean for things to go like this.'

Anger surged inside him. He wanted to yell and shout and just tell her to leave, but part of his heart was still responding to her every word. Hoping and praying that pieces of what she'd said might be true.

He sighed and ran his fingers through his hair. He met her gaze. 'You can't do this to me, Skye. It's not fair.'

She reached over and took his hand, threading her fingers through his. 'I watched two people earlier, telling themselves that they had no regrets. That they wanted to spend every moment together, in sickness and health.' She put her other hand to her heart again. 'And what I knew right away was that if I didn't get on a plane, to tell you, face to face, exactly how I felt, I would regret it for the rest of my life.'

She squeezed the fingers that were threaded with hers. 'I love you, Jay Bannerman. Probably from that first time you kissed me. It didn't matter that you'd been grumpy, it didn't matter you'd pushed people away. I got that. I understood. I just didn't understand myself.' She took a deep breath. 'But I hope that I do now. Tell me to go away. Tell me I ruined things and that it's all my fault. But just know that I made a mistake. And I'll always regret it, no matter what the future holds.'

Jay had been listening. Really listening. It was so easy to let his defences fall automatically back into place. It would be even easier to shut himself off the way he'd done for the last year.

But the last six weeks of his life had been different. For the first time in a long time he'd glimpsed happiness. He hadn't wanted to acknowledge it, but he wasn't a fool. Would he really let her walk back out of his life?

He took a shaky breath. 'I don't want to have a life with regrets either.' He straightened his shoulders. 'But I can't go back and forth. I love you, Skye. And you broke my heart this morning, you made me feel as if I'd read things all wrong between us. Because I've felt the heat between us too. You know I didn't want to date another colleague, you know I didn't want to do anything that would make me the talk of the hospital. But then I met you, and all those good intentions went out the window. I've spent the last few hours feeling like an absolute fool.'

She winced as he kept talking in a low voice. 'Neither of us knows what the future holds. I live in London, you live in Edinburgh. I don't even know how we'll make that work. But I'm willing to give it a try. I'm willing to see where this goes.'

A frown crept across her face.

He was surprised. He'd thought she'd be happy, but she turned to face him, pulling him a bit closer.

'No,' she said firmly. 'I don't want to see where this goes. I want more than that. I want the whole shebang. I want a happily ever after. If I have to move to make that happen, then I will. I want to be with you.'

'You do?' His dark eyes were wide, a smile finally hinting at the edge of his mouth. Was he willing to take this jump? Yes, without a shadow of a doubt.

She gave a smile as she wound her hands up around his neck, brushing her lips against his. 'We might be taking it a little too fast, but I do.'

EPILOGUE

Christmas Eve, one year later

'WHERE ARE WE GOING?'

'It's a surprise.' Jay winked. He pulled into a rural estate with a large grand house tucked behind Arthur's Seat in Edinburgh.

She shot him a glance. 'Did you invite your parents here for Christmas? My mum? Is that what you're up to?'

Skye had no idea what was going on. Things between them had just got better and better. As his last act in Edinburgh, he'd given approval for the next stage of the project. It had only taken two months for him to transfer up to Edinburgh on a permanent basis, and they'd been working together ever since.

Did people talk about them in the hospital? Probably. But only to say how sickeningly happy they both seemed.

As they pulled up in front of the grand white

house, Skye could see the main hallway fes-
tooned with red decorations. As she stepped
out the car, Jay couldn't hide the big smile on
his face.

'What have you done?' she asked again, feeling very suspicious.

They walked inside and Jay's parents, his sister and her partner, and Skye's mum and her
charming boyfriend were waiting for them. Skye
let out a squeal and hugged them all. 'You're all
here for Christmas!' she exclaimed.

She adored Jay's parents and his sister, and
her mum was now settled with the fellow widower she'd met in Spain. She narrowed her gaze
as she saw them all exchange glances.

Jay's voice at the back of her neck startled her.
'Not exactly,' he said.

She turned around and he was down on one
knee, box already opened towards her. 'You told
me you wanted a happily ever after, that you
didn't want to wait to see where this goes.' He
was beaming. 'Will you marry me?'

Skye let out a squeal. 'Of course I will.' She
hugged him around the neck, then jumped up
and down as he slid the elegant diamond on her
finger.

He was still down on one knee as he surprised

her once again. 'You know I don't want a long engagement?'

'What?' she asked, a little confused. 'Well, yes, I know that.'

He stood up. 'Good. So how do you feel about getting married today?'

For a moment her legs were like jelly. 'What?'

She looked at the faces around her. All of them beaming, just like Jay's. 'You're all in on it, aren't you?' she asked, pretending to frown even though she couldn't stop smiling.

Jay pulled a face for a second. 'You can shout at me later, but I might have posted the notice about our wedding in the hope you would actually say yes.'

Her mum gave a shrug. 'I might even have picked you a dress,' she said, her voice a bit shaky.

Skye enveloped her in a big hug. 'Oh, thank you.' Everything was falling into place for her. The one thing she'd always known she'd miss at her wedding was her father's presence. But here, now? Doing it this way meant she didn't have time to think about it, or to wallow. The fact that Jay had obviously enlisted her mother's help for her dress was just perfect. And she absolutely trusted her mother's taste.

'You've organised all this?' She tilted her head as she looked at Jay.

'Well,' he admitted, nodding to a woman in the corner with a clipboard. 'Maddie has actually played a big part.'

Maddie stepped up. 'If you're ready, Ms Campbell, I'll take you up to your room to get ready.'

Her stomach gave an excited flip. They were really doing this. Right now, in this gorgeous venue, at her favourite time of year.

He couldn't have planned this more perfectly.

Half an hour later, Skye stood blinking at the mirror in her Audrey Hepburn styled, smooth boat-necked dress. It had a nipped in waistline and a three-quarter-length skirt in pale satin.

'I couldn't have picked better,' she murmured to her mother, who handed her the bridal bouquet of off-season orange gardenias, paired with dark green leaves. She felt something against her palm and lifted the bouquet to inspect it.

A silver chain was wound around the stems, with the words *With you always*, coupled with a small photo of her dad in a silver locket.

She let out a sob.

Her mother wrapped her arms around her. 'This is meant to be a happy day.'

'It is,' she said, tears flowing down her face. 'I would have always wanted Dad to be part of this, and this is just perfect.'

'Are we ready then?' asked her mum. She'd changed into an elegant dark green dress and jacket—she even had a fascinator in her hair.

Skye gave a nod and checked her make-up, covering the tear tracks and putting on a lipstick that matched her flowers. Her heart was singing.

Everything was perfect. A beautiful venue. The man that she loved. The people that were important to them both. And the best time of year. Jay Bannerman knew her. Every part of her.

She would have hated the fuss and worry of a big wedding. She would have fretted about who to invite. How to arrange time off. Now, it was all done for her.

She wasn't even going to tell them that she might have glimpsed the wedding notification a month ago, when they'd been selling their houses, buying a new one together and sorting out insurances. Skye was a doctor—she'd never sign anything without paying attention and reading every piece of paper on her desk. But everything about this was perfect.

She took a last glance in the mirror, then

opened the door, her mum beside her, and made her way along the corridor to the main stairs.

Their wedding venue was a beautiful room at the back of the house that looked over the snow-covered gardens.

As she walked in, she let out a gasp as she saw their celebrant. It was Connie, their receptionist from the ward.

Both Jay and Connie shot her conspiratorial glances. Connie was wearing a beautiful navy dress.

'I've been training,' Connie admitted. 'Only Jay knew. This is my first wedding.'

Jay was in a traditional Irish kilt in shades of green and a black Argyll jacket. Skye couldn't stop beaming. She leaned over and whispered in his ear. 'You look spectacular. And at some point, I'll kill you for all this, but right now, I'm just so happy.'

'You're stunning,' he whispered back as he kissed her cheek. 'And your mum couldn't have picked you a more perfect dress.'

They clasped hands as Connie started the ceremony. It didn't take long for her to invite them to talk.

'We have the option of traditional wedding vows at a ceremony, and, if things are planned in advance, sometimes brides and grooms like to write their own. But...' she smiled broadly '...we know that one bride didn't get a chance to do that. However, I'd still like to give them an opportunity to tell each other why marriage is right for them.'

They faced each other and Jay held both of her hands whilst looking her in the eye. 'A year ago today, I got together with the person who was made for me. That's the way I like to think of it. When Skye and I first met, there were sparks, but not all good ones. Anyone would think I annoyed her?'

Their family members laughed as he continued. 'But as we got to know each other, I found it hard to resist Miss Sunshine, as she's known at the hospital. Skye Campbell, I love you. You have the biggest heart, the best attitude and are one of the best and most caring doctors I've ever worked with. Your research is your heart, and everyone knows it. But I hope that I have a little of your heart too.'

She gave him the biggest smile.

He continued. 'I can't imagine what my life would be like if I hadn't met you. You're the first thing I think about when I wake up in the morning, and the last thing I think about at night. And most of those times—work willing—I get to be beside you. You make me see the better side of life. Everything I do with you is fun—no matter what it is. Because we both know how precious minutes are. So, I stand here today, saying the words in sickness and in health, because we both know how important they are.'

Skye's lips started trembling. Her heart was so full it could explode. She pulled Jay's hands up to her heart.

'Dr Grumpy,' she started. 'Jay Bannerman. The man who walked into my life with only work on his mind. I'm so glad you came to Scotland, I'm so glad we got to work together. But most of all, I'm so glad we got to know each other, because those first weeks were the best thing that ever happened to me. You gave me confidence and supported me to talk in front of hundreds of people. You believed in me when I didn't believe in myself. And when I panicked, and ran,' she gave him a smile, 'you forgave me, and told me you loved me.' She reached over and touched his face. 'You are my happily ever after, Jay. And I can't wait for "for ever" to start.'

And, with that, he embraced her, leaned her back and kissed her as their families cheered them on.

* * * * *